For Mandy +

Tony Chapman

JOKES
AND
OTHER LIES

Short Stories

Tony Chapman

First Published 1994 by
MINERVA PRESS
2, Old Brompton Road,
London SW7 3DQ.

Printed in Great Britain by
Antony Rowe, Chippenham, Wiltshire.

JOKES
AND
OTHER LIES

Cover Design

By

ROGER BARSON

ACKNOWLEDGEMENTS

"I wish to thank all the knowns
and unknowns who originated some of the jokes
around which these stories have been written.
Without their help, I could have only told lies."

Tony Chapman

" You canNOT be serious! "

John McEnroe

CONTENTS

THE JOKEMAN

Approaching the yellow streetlights surrounding the airbase, Eric decides to leave the road and head out across the desert. The air hangs in his face like a warm blanket. And, even in the predawn gloom, Eric can see that the parched earth is grey, cracked. He thinks his tongue probably looks much the same way. It certainly feels that way. Laughter still trickles inside him. God, what a night!

It had been a night of hours and hours, of days, of days and nights, of months of days and nights. Or so it seems to Eric now. His stomach is sore from laughter, his ears still hot, his brain overloaded. It was a night filled with jokes. And now, smack on cue, WHAMMO, it's dawn. Dawn, thinks Eric, the punch line of night. A thin, raw, reddish line that rips across the horizon before him. Bringing a smile to his lips as the sky opens up, he sincerely believes, for him alone.

Three hours or so later, the sky cloudless, pretty as in pictures, Eric still stumbles onwards feeling much the same only hotter. He looks up and catches the briefest glimpse of a shadow. It's thick and dense black, dense and quick. And it's right upon him like an umbrella opening over his head. But it's far too quick for that and it's followed instantly by a swift, fierce pain as an extraordinary force flattens him ruthlessly into the desert crust. Breaking the crisp surface, splitting skin and flesh, snapping bone, crushing organs, killing.

Detective Irving "Hambone" Griggs surveys the ruins of Eric and the charred, shattered remains of another man, as yet unknown, who appears to be clutching a cast iron gas stove. As Hambone will freely admit, it never is a pretty sight but, ugliness aside, this is a rum one if ever he's seen it.

He'd spotted the crater and the debris as he was routinely patrolling the Cross Desert Highway. Being a romantic, his first thoughts ran to UFOs or at least to a satellite that had come unglued from its path across the heavens. But no, it's another bloody death. Two in truth. And it means that some very pragmatic investigative work has dropped cleanly in his lap. So, overcoming an instinctive and somewhat urgent desire to vomit, with his usual professional aplomb, Hambone radios for assistance.

"And, my God, do I need it."

His first problem is, of course, the obvious problem. What the hell happened here? This problem is compounded by one very obvious other fact: something is missing here. And that something is a second set of footprints leading to the crater. A set that should, by rights, be deeply embedded in the desert when you take into account the weight of this stove that the man was carrying. But there's nothing to be seen, save the merest traces of Eric's earthshoes that have barely scratched the surface, hardly creased the crust.

"N, n, n, n, n, ... I" says Hambone and slowly lifts his face towards the sky. He's hoping against all hope to discover, say, the branch of a sturdy tree, the boom of a crane or maybe even a high diving or spring board which might remain from the time when the desert was a lake and the now empty Cross Desert Highway teemed with cars packed to capacity with keen aquatic sports persons. But no. Which leaves Hambone with the one and only option and it's staring right back into his staring face. Of course. He came, with his cargo, from the sky. His fall, meteoric in nature, broken only by Eric.

Hambone decides to call the airbase and check on all flights that have taken place in the last few hours. Meanwhile, assistance is making its way towards him in the shape of two little clouds of dust containing an ambulance and another patrol car. He waits, motionless, mystified as to (among many other things) why a man would jump from a plane holding a gas stove, an antiquated gas stove at that.

Because he has to begin somewhere, Hambone elects to make what he expects to be his most unpleasant and difficult call. Having ascertained who Eric is from an extremely compressed wallet in his inside jacket pocket and being clueless still as to the identity of the other man, he calls Eric's wife. Amazingly, it results in little or no pain or anguish whatsoever. The woman is sorry to hear the news. She's sorry but not unduly sad. Indeed she isn't even duly sad. Hambone immediately arranges to meet her.

The door of the mobile home, built in 1956 of stainless steel and having lost its lustre long ago, opens on an almost indifferent "Oh," followed finally by an almost apologetic "Mmmmm."

"Mrs. Smedley?" offers Hambone with a sympathetic smile and proffers his badge.

"Medley." The voice is firm, gin-soaked but firm. "Do come in. Don't stand there on the doorstep making the place look untidy."

Hambone follows her bulky shape into the dark, cool interior of the trailer. An ancient air conditioning unit rattles relentlessly and everything feels a little damp.

"May I call you 'Hambone', Mister Griggs? Sorry, 'Detective'."

Hambone has never been, as they say, backward in coming forward and he quickly picks up on her playful manner. "That was 'Detective' not 'defective', now wasn't it, Mrs Smedley-Medley? You're a One, I can tell. You're a joker, aren't you? I can tell a joker, Mrs..."

"Nothing, nothing could be further from the truth. Nothing. Get that straight in your head, right now. Right from the start." What a change in the woman! She's frozen rigid. There's venom here. The voice as cold as Christmas. Then suddenly, she reverts to her former almost girlish self. "No, Hambone, not I. My husband now ... well, he was the joker of the family. He prided himself on being what he called a Jokeman. Like his friend Ernie. They loved jokes, you see. And I take that to be a 'yes' to 'Hambone', right Hambone?"

"A 'yes' to 'Hambone' it is, Mrs..."

"Call me Doris, Eric always did. And come sit here by me on the love seat, Hambone. Come do. It's for two. Come." Imperious now, the tone. She throws back her head, hair as brittle as a Brillo pad, and draws her ruby lips tight across her ruined teeth. She could be 58, she could possibly be 44, but she could never be what she really is. She's really 37.

"Now Doris!" Hambone is flustered but he's not going to let her see that. He's staying where he is by the outer door in a kitchen chair beside a huge, pale pink velveteen labrador.

"Come, Hambone!" It's an order.

Hambone crosses his legs and smiles a knowing smile. It doesn't work. He tries another tack. It's an appeal to the woman in her.

"Now, Doris, what do you think my little Pork Chop would make of that if she were here to hear us? Mmmm?"

"Huh?" Her eyes, glassy, glaze frostily.

"The little woman, my wife, my dear Ethel..."

"Hmm. We do like our meats now don't we? Carnivores all, eh, Hambone?"

"Huh?"

"Who gives a damn, Hambone? Wives, husbands, lovers ... who cares? They're only ... they're only ... people." She spits the word across the darkness.

"Well, Doris, I suppose that is the question....."

"Questions, questions ..." she drifts off, quietly now.

Another change. Hambone's having trouble keeping up here.

"Yes."

"Hambone. 'Hambone'. I love that name."

"Yes, Doris. 'Doris' is a nice name, too."

"Hate it, hate it, hate it."

"Yes," says Hambone, ignoring this latest metamorphosis, "and so is..." he pauses and the pause appears to unwind her somewhat, releasing whatever tension she coiled up inside herself.

" .... so is ...'Eric'."

"Yes, Eric," says Doris, lighting a slimmer-than-slim cigarette with absentminded charmlessness.

"Tell me more."

"What can I tell you?"

"Well, tell me something, Doris. So far ..." Hambone clears his throat with a tiny cough. He's a big man with a big neck and the teeny cough is ludicrous, "... so far you haven't really told me anything."

"You know all you need to know about Eric, Hambone."

"What is it that I know exactly, Doris?"

"................"

"Perhaps you could tell me again."

" ...."

"Now I have my notebook out and..."

Doris blows a column of smoke at the ceiling and with vast contempt utters the single word, "Jokeman." Hambone waits, he needs more. More is necessary to continue this investigation. More is not coming. "Do you, Doris, mean by that what I think you mean that by that I think...?"

"..............."

"You mean he was a joke ... ?"

"..............."

"... as a man?"

"He was a Jokeman, Hambone. You're a policeman, Harry is a fireman, Jim is a furrier, Me I'm a ... forget me. Eric is, was a Jokeman. Can I put it plainer? He loved jokes. He and his friend Ernie. He more than Ernie, in fact. They called themselves Jokemen because they loved jokes. No joke, Hambone. Eric lived for jokes. I told him. I told him they'd be the death of him. I warned him. And did he listen? Did he heed the warnings? Did he? You're the policeman, you tell me."

"Well, Doris ... "

"Come along, Hambone, spill the beans. What the hell happened? He's dead, right? Why, Hambone? You're the detective, Hambone? Do I have to do your work for you,

Hambone? .... Oh I do like that name ... "

"Frankly, Doris, we are in no position as yet to release any statement as to the cause, possible or otherwise, of your ... "

"Frankly, Hambone, I always hated them."

"Doris? Who, Doris?"

"I said, 'Hambone' I ... mmm, does it, perchance, refer to anything ... er, personal ... something ... about your person? I said I hated jokes. All my life I've hated jokes."

"Well, as a woman, in your position ... "

"Let me tell you something, Sunbeam. I take my sex seriously. I don't see anything funny in my sex. I don't want to hear anything funny. It isn't funny. You understand? 'Cos if you don't understand that, Hambone, you know nothing about me and there's no point continuing this discussion one second longer. You understand?"

"I understand perfectly, Doris. And did Eric understand?"

" ...."

"I mean did Eric know this .... ?"

"Eric knew what Eric knew."

Hambone seizes this new line as if his life, professional and private, depended on it.

"The point is, Doris, did he know something that might have caused or inadvertently led to his untimely demise?"

"His... Untimely! Demise!"

"Yes, Doris ..." Hambone now adopts the sympathetic approach. It's an appeal to the human being in her.

"Just what are you getting at, Buster?"

"The cause of death, Doris ... the cause. Nothing more, nothing less, Doris." His voice is soft, velvety as the dog by his chair.

"When, Hambone, are you going to get this into your sexy face, your stupifyingly stud-like features? Be the stud you are, Hambone. The stud I take you for and I will take you for, Hambone. The man lived for jokes and died for one, by one. Call it what you will. Don't ask me. I never understood a joke in my life, Hambone. Never saw the point in them.

Waste of breath. Now, come join me on the love seat, won't you?"

During this little speech, Doris opened and closed her legs so many times Hambone, who was counting, actually did lose count. And now she sits, her hands thrust into the apricot coloured skirt of her dress, pushing it down tight between her thighs. Hambone takes a deep breath in the hope it will prevent a blush. Fat chance. Crimson, he stares into his note book, his pants bulging. This must stop. Her eyes, no longer frosted glass, are glowing madly in the dark.

"T..tell me .. about last night."

"Last night?" The horror show is back, she's glaring furiously. "What d'you expect to hear? You want to hear about a night of what? Of passion? Of wild sex? Of animal lust? Of hot, sticky stuff like that? Don't make me laugh, Hambone. I haven't laughed in years. That's the truth. It's a joke, Hambone. It's no laughing matter." Suddenly, she looks like she might cry.

"I'm sorry, Doris. I know this must be hard for you .."

"Ooooh, hard, Hambone, I like it hard. And all he did was tell jokes. With his friend Ernie. Ernie came over, what?, about five-ish ..." Doris opens her legs again, throwing back her head, then regaining her composure, lights another slim cigarette. A funny, plump little figure with a thin little stick burning in her pudgy fingers.

"Please, Doris, I've a job to do here ... "

"Shut up, Hambone, will you? Just shut up for a minute ... And listen. They told jokes, jokes only Jokemen laugh at and they laughed and laughed and laughed and I went to bed and I heard the laughter, on and on into the night, and then Ernie left and Eric said (to no-one in particular) that he needed air. He could hardly speak, his voice had gone with all his joke telling and all his laughing, you should have heard the laughter, you've heard nothing like it, I bet. And off he goes. That's all there is to it, Hambone."

She looks at him with a kind of longing as if a wash of

tenderness has passed over her in the damp darkness of the trailer. They sit in silence for minutes.

"OK., Hambone, get this." The firmness is back.

"OK., Doris."

"Mention was made, just before he left, I was awake still, of a plane. Ernie was talking, I don't know, I wasn't listening. But I remember a plane. Find the pilot of that plane, Hambone. Find the pilot." Her voice, seerlike, ghostlike now. "Find the pilot."

"The pilot," says Hambone, foolishly.

"............" says Doris, inscrutably.

"............"

"It's a joke, you see. Knowing Eric, it has to be." She's deadly serious now. "Now, join me on the love seat and let me get to know Hambone a lot, lot better. I'd like that. So don't be shy, come now!"

Miraculously, Sam Kite had survived the fall. Yes, he was going to die and it wasn't going to be long before he did but for the present Sam was alive, if not kicking. He can, however, speak, lying in a hospital bed at the airbase which Hambone Griggs finally got around to calling.

Hambone arrives hot, sweaty, red-faced and riddled with guilt and rage. It is the sweat, guilt and rage of a much loved husband who has committed adultery with the widow of a man into whose death the aforesaid husband is inquiring in the name of the law and common decency. And that widow had not so much as smiled throughout the whole damn thing.

"Aaaaaargh!" says Hambone.

"May I help you, Detective? And a good afternoon to you," says the hospital receptionist in a quiet, well rehearsed manner.

"Aaaaaaargh!" he repeats.

"Something the matter, Detective?"

"This way, Detective," calls a doctor, possibly saving the receptionist's life. "Look sharp. He hasn't got long." He ushers Hambone down a bile green corridor.

"Aaaaaaargh!" says Hambone on the run.

The doctor opens the door into a room painted the same bile green and containing one small iron cot. The mess in the cot stirs briefly. It is Sam Kite. Sam: the one and only pilot of the one and only Belvedere Blue Jay. The Belvedere Blue Jay: the one and only thing Sam Kite had ever built in his entire life of 67 years. It was named, in part, for his late wife Harriet Belvedere and in part for his favourite baseball team, the Toronto Blue Jays. Harriet's Belvedere millions had provided the funds and the Blue Jays' success, the inspiration. And now the Belvedere Blue Jay lies scattered in several thousand pieces in the hills some four miles north of where what's left of Sam Kite lies in a tiny hospital bed. Both have bits missing, bits that are lost and gone forever, both Sam and the BBJ.

Sam had bailed out at almost 20,000 feet above the desert after the Belvedere Blue Jay had quite unaccountably barrel-rolled and refused to be righted. Sam hated flying upside down and also foresaw hideous problems awaiting him when the time came to land. So, with a tear, a prayer, a fond farewell and a well-packed parachute, Sam and the Belvedere Blue Jay were parted.

His fall, as previously stated, was nothing short of miraculous. Unable to open the well-packed parachute, he plummeted 19,869 feet into assorted shrubs, bushes and newly planted trees on the perimeter of the airbase. Here he was found by a Mexican gardener who declared Sam to be Lucifer Incarnate and who had immediately called for a priest and the military police.

"Hambone Griggs," says Hambone, still hot and furious with himself.

"Sam Kite," says Sam miraculously.

"Must say, it's a miracle you're still with us," says Hambone, trying not to look at the bundle of bandages and tubes on the bed.

"Do you think so?". Sam sounds surprised.

"Tell me all you can," says Hambone ignoring the man's

feelings and taking out his note pad and sitting in the one chair in the room. The doctor leaves with a warning not to overstretch Mr. Kite.

"Well," says Sam, "there was this flash of light, very intense beneath me as I fell and an enormous WHUUUMP sound."

"Your plane?"

"No, no, no Hamstring, a house. A house, couldn't be far from here actually, thinking about it ... "

" Bone. Hambone."

" ... exploding. That's what. Exploding in a flash of light and an enormous WHUUUMP sound. Blinding. Deafening. Fetlock, Hemlock .. "

"Hambone," says Hambone wearily.

"Right. And dammit, you know what? Of course you don't know or you wouldn't be asking now would you, pay attention Kitey," says Kite into his bandages. "You wouldn't believe it. I had trouble and I was there, for heaven's sake, but coming up at me, at tremendous speed, tremendous velocity, is this figure, black he was, not Black black but.... charred. And you know what? Course you don't. This charred figure is clutching do you believe ... a stove of some kind? Do you believe that?"

"I believe that, Mr. Kite. I believe."

"Racing up, like he's been shot from a cannon, he is. And I think 'Kitey, something's up, here', something strange, know what I mean Boney?"

"This has got to be a joke," says Hambone into his pad.

"No joke. Here I am falling at 32 ft. per sec per sec or whatever and here he is rising at God knows what ft. per.

"And as we pass in mid air at approximately 8,000 feet, a guess but I couldn't be far off at that, as we pass, I shout to him: 'I say, old boy, do you happen to know anything about parachutes?' I was desperate, you understand."

"I understand," says Hambone who plainly doesn't.

"And, bugger me, d'you know what? He looks back at me ... he was a plumber I would say ... he looks at me and he says, "No I don't. Do you know anything about gas stoves?"

Hambone looks up from his pad. The old boy, from what he can see of him, is perfectly serious. He's not making this up, who would?

"So we go our separate ways. No choice in the matter. But, God, Bonehead I could have died laughing at the time. Almost did, of course. What a joke, eh?"

"It's no joke, Mr. Kite," says Hambone rising from the chair.

"Sorry you see it that way, Hamfist ... "

Hambone is gone, he's out in the corridor and on his way. Case closed, near enough.

"Of course it is, Hamster, of course it is ..." Kite's voice reverberates off the painted walls and out to the reception desk of the hospital.

"Of course it is."

"GLORIOUS"

Let me tell you: I'm sick and tired of animal, fish and fowl stories. No matter how delightful the delivery, no matter how witty the plot and the punchline, no, I have had it up to here, up to the beak, you might say, with the whole bloody lot of them. And, take it from me, there are a bloody hell of a lot of them. I mean, aren't you sick of them, too?

Having myself been the original model and hero of two of the very best parrot jokes ever, I can tell you something else. It's not as much fun as you might think, being a star. Really. And as for fame: well, it's a Curate's Egg if you ask me. The good parts, well, they're pretty obvious. The not so good .... well, take my present position.

Today, I happen to be the parrot of the renowned hostelry, The Parrot and Chips. No, not the nicest nor the most inviting name to give a pub, to my mind anyhow, but memorable, yes it is memorable. That I admit. And it is to this that I have ... risen, soared, even. This is how far fame has flung me. Amazing, eh? Fortune, on the other hand, went to my previous owner/manager. Isn't that so often the case in such matters? He is now, the sod, basking like the beached whale he resembles, by his pool beneath the Mediterranean sun at his villa in Marbella. May he rot. And he's probably still dining out on the Plumber-who's-come-to-mend-the-pipes and the Zoo-or-no-Zoo jokes. Both mine. Both me, through and through. 100% and don't you forget it, friend. Hey, ho! What can I tell you?

Anyway, the point is, I'm stuck here at the end of the Long Bar, chained to my perch with the clear instruction, in caps, DO NOT FEED! Some people, thank goodness, ignore it. If they didn't I'd be dead by now. I'd have starved to death long since on what they feed me here. Despite my status and pulling power. Oh yes, I still can draw the crowds, no matter what anyone says. Forgive me, I digress.

At the end of this bar, believe me, I have heard jokes and stories, bad and worse, day after day, night after night for almost a year now. The only thing preventing me from ripping out some of these people's tongues is my chain and the only thing that is saving me from certain madness is the playing of the Glorias, on banjo and piano every evening. Ah, the sound itself is like nothing else I know and, on top of that, they drown out the jokes.

This is their story.

I knew it, I just knew it, the moment he set foot in the bar. You can tell, you know, when you've been in the business, as it were, as long as I have. I spotted him immediately as a joke teller. A story teller if ever you saw one. Not bad looking as it happened. For what he was. And a great one with the words. Oh yes, the gift he had all right, of the gab as they call it.

(Tell me, do I ever sound Irish at all, to you? Tell me if I do. Because I'm not. And it could just be the Irish jokes they are so fond of relating that I could be picking up the accent. So lilting it is, don't you think? And that's another thing, by the way. One good thing about my last owner/manager: he did cure me of the swearing. God, I swore like a trooper, I did. Living with that vicar did it, you know. Of course you know.)

So in he walks and in no time they're all agog, locals, regulars and strangers alike, even Jimmy the Barman, the shit, ooops! apologies, but I cannot abide the bastard, which he is by the way, I have it on unimpeachable authority, believe me. I do believe the owner of the place had a hand, or another part of his anatomy, in it and that's why he's employed, for crying out loud. Certainly, it's not for his charm or personality or even for his skills behind the bar. But enough of that. My position here gets more precarious as time goes by, you understand. How many jokes have you heard about a parrot in a bar? I have to be careful. Watch my tongue.

Funny how fast folk forget, isn't it?

Anyway, or any road up as my feathered friends up north are likely to say, back to our hero, the travelling salesman, for that is what he is by trade. And Harris is his name, as in tweed which, indeed, he was wearing at the time.

"Never forget a name, never forget a face." That was his phrase. No, wait, the other way around it was.

"Never forget a face ..." Then the name.

Yes, that was it. Because he followed it with a rather weak, in my opinion, "Mine's Harris, what's yours?" And then there would be a "Well, I'll have a Bitter" or the respondent wouldn't be so pushy and say his or her name. Pitiful, I agree, but a way of saying hello, I suppose. And most people are lonely, or so it seems to me. I mean, I can understand why. They are so dreadfully dull for the most part. And when they're not dull they're arseholes, sorry, done it again. But they are, you know. Brash, loud, arrogant, you know. Like my new owner/manager, Willis. Another you-know-what.

Anyway, he walks in and he buys drinks and he starts cracking jokes, regular jokes. He avoids ethnic jokes, I notice. He's not stupid. He hasn't sussed out his audience yet. Then, oh yes, it had to happen. It always does when you aren't sure what you can get away with. The animal, fish and fowl stories begin. Well, he has his audience entranced, I have to say. He's leading them by the nose. But, as always, audiences get tired. And he starts out on what must be his fifteenth combination bar/animal, fish or fowl joke.

I'll tell you what it was, if you like. I mean, it was one of the better ones. It involved a man, you guessed, walking into a bar, yes, with a newt on his shoulder. Bet that got you, huh? Weren't expecting a newt eh? So he walks in and he asks the barman, who is a similar creature to our very own Jimmy in terms of intelligence, wit and repartee, for a drink, a beer. And the barman serves it up. And he says, "Excuse me, but I think you have something on your shoulder there, fella."

And the man says, "Yes, I have."

The barman says, "Hey, fella, I said I think you got somefing on yer shoulder."

And the guy says he knows and tells him it's his newt.

"A NEWT! Whatsat!!!?? Some kinda pet or somefing?"

"Well, yes, he is some kind of pet as it happens."

"Oh, I see. So ..." says the barman, looking round for support, "I suppose we 'ave a name for 'im, do we?"

"Well, yes we do. Yes, we do."

"I see me old cocker, so what's 'is name, then?"

"I call him 'Tiny', since you ask," says the man, taking a sip of his beer.

"I see," says the barman, but of course he doesn't, "you call him 'Tiny'. Why do you call 'im 'Tiny'?"

"Well, I call him 'Tiny' because he's my newt."

"I don't get it," says the barman. But everybody in the bar does. Both in the bar here and in the joke. However, like I said, the crowd was getting tired and was beginning to turn ugly, which they can so quickly. A combination of tiredness and alcohol will do it every time, I've noticed.

As it happens, Harris is saved by the Glorias who start to play at that very moment. Harris doesn't pay them any attention to begin with. He's too busy trying to make friends with people. Now that he can't tell jokes, for no-one could hear even if anyone wanted to which they didn't, he's busy buying drinks for everyone. A sickening piece of behaviour, pitiful, really. It's called buying friends, I know. But they like it and he doesn't seem to mind (must be on commission and doing well). It's all so superficial, of course. But then, aren't most things when it comes to human behaviour? I mean, why get involved when you don't have to?

Then the Glorias run into a real rip-snorter. It's a really rousing rendition of "She'll be coming round the mountain when she comes". Always makes me laugh, that tune, for some reason. Can't think why. I can even feel a bit of a smile coming on now, just thinking about it. Funny, that. Now, whether or not it has that effect on Harris, I really can't say. But it certainly got his attention at the time.

"My word," he says between clenched teeth.

"My word," he says again. "And who might they be?"

As it happens, the old fart next to him is a regular. "The Glorias," he growls. "Cheers!" he adds, downing in one gulp the Scotch Harris had bought him and turning back to his pint of flat Bitter.

"Glorious!' says Harris.

"Glorias," says the old fart.

"Glorious!" says Harris again. Maybe he hasn't heard the man.

"Not Glorious. Glori-as. The Glori-as."

"Yes, yes I know. And they're glorious."

"I suppose they might be," says the fart with a scowl, "if that's your cup of tea. If that's what turns you on, as they say. Tragic, I call it. And I just hope, young man, you aren't taking the mickey ... because if you are, I'll take you outside....."

Harris can't understand what the devil the old fool's on about. He sees everything through a fine mist. The mist clears at the mention of being taken outside. "Mmmm, what? No I'm not joking. I think they are glorious. I mean it. Believe me, I do really." And then Harris understands. He sees that the girls are no ordinary twin sisters. They are, yes, Siamese twins. And they are joined at the neck and at the hip. Which is a bit weird, thinks Harris, but quite wonderful, nevertheless. "What do they normally drink, do you happen to know, by any chance?"

"They usually drink gin and tonics," the old man replies.

"Two gins, large, and tonics, Jimmy, if you please."

Well, the Glorias are thrilled. Harris is charming, he's courteous and, on top of everything else, he keeps the gins, large, and tonics coming. And he continues to buy drinks for the crowd at the bar. So everybody's happy. And the evening quite whizzes by.

Come closing time, Harris offers to drive the girls home. We know what that means, don't we? No question about it. We know what that means, O.K. I mean, it's so obvious what he is after. But, like I said, the Glorias are totally enamoured with the man. Totally.

And, believe it or not, they have the time of their sweet young lives. They have a fantastic time. Harris, naturally, is brilliant in bed. All this I overhear the Glorias telling their friend Freda, who works in the Snug, the following evening. They are beside themselves with joy.

"He kept shouting 'Glorious! Glorious!' all night. What a riot! And what a gentleman! Made us breakfast in bed and everything."

They went on and on and on about the guy. About what a stud he was. About the size of his dick and the places he put it. I don't know, really I don't. Those girls! Who'd have thought, to look at them? And the orgasms, of course. We had to hear all about them. Because of their condition, because of what they are, if one had an orgasm, the other felt it too. So they went on orgasming all night bloody long. I got quite horny, myself, thinking about that as they talked to Freda.

Anyhow (I notice I say that quite a lot, don't I) anyhow (like I was saying) Harris promises them that he will be back very soon to see them. Obviously, because of his job, he has to leave but he'll be back "very soon" he says. Mmmm.

Say what you will but orgasms do do things for women, don't they? I noticed the change in the Glorias. Their skins even looked different. Sort of cleaner, fresher somehow. And their eyes, that old chestnut about there being a twinkle in the eyes, yes, well, it's true. It was true about them, at least. And, my, you should have heard them play that following evening. The ballads were dreamier, the sad songs sadder, the loud songs louder, everything heightened, you could say. They even got to that Philistine, Jimmy. That's how effectively they played.

I couldn't help noticing, however, they kept glancing at the door everytime it swung open. But no. No Harris tonight. Nor tomorrow night, nor the next night, nor the next. Weeks passed, in fact. Months passed and there was no sign of the man.

Things pretty soon got very much back to normal at the Parrot and Chips, I tell you. I mean, we knew it would happen, didn't we? (You knew, didn't you?) Oh yes. It was, well, just one of those things. The girls knew, too, I suspect, deep down. The man had no intention of returning. But no-one mentioned his name and the Glorias couldn't help occasionally glancing wistfully towards the door as they played, night after night after night.

It must have been almost a year later, within about half an hour or so to go to closing time, that the door opens and, bugger me, if it isn't our man, Harris. And, ignoring the music, he strides straight up to the bar and starts buying drinks.

The banjo player nudges her sister and says (I can hear her from here), "Guess what the cat brought in."

"What cat? We have a parrot. We don't have a cat."

"It's just a saying, isn't it?"

"I don't know."

"Well, guess anyway. Guess who just strode in."

"I don't know."

"I know you don't know. Stop saying that and guess."

"Who?"

"Him."

"Who?" the piano player's obviously chosen to forget the whole incident.

"Him!"

"Oh." She remembers.

"Well?"

"Well, what?" She remembers, but she's distanced the memory. She's not going to let it affect her now.

"Well," says the banjo player, "shouldn't we ask him to join us, no pun intended? Then we could maybe buy him a drink or something."

"Nah!" says the piano player, cool as can be. "Best not. He probably doesn't remember us."

I damn-near fell off my perch, I tell you. Who could forget

them, these glorious girls, glorious girls who provide us with glorious music night after night? Who? And just as I'm thinking that, you know what? In walks this dog, a large black mongrel, and he casually strolls up to the bar. And I hear, "Never forget a face. Never forget a name. Mine's Harris. What's yours?" And I hear the dog reply that he'd appreciate a double brandy which, in itself, was very odd because he usually has a vodka.......

THE GIFT

"What do you mean, this story has been around for over twenty years?"

"What I say, Brian."

"But it's new to us, isn't it? And we're the only ones who've been told about it, right?"

"Right, Brian. But think about it, love, think. It has been around for years. In fact, it's 21 today, in case you've forgotten already. I mean, Jesus Christ, Brian, this is one of the greatest stories since, well, Jesus Christ, Brian. When you think about it."

"What are you talking about, Hector?"

Hector and Brian are waiting in the reception area of an extremely large and extremely quiet office of the famous property company, Thomsen London, PLC.

"I don't believe you, Brian, sometimes. Really I don't. I mean can't you see what this is? It's a bloody amazing story. It's gonna make History. It's so fantastic that it's incredible, Brian. Can't you see that?"

"Hector, you're getting excited. Just relax, will you?"

"Relax, he says," says Hector. "I tell you, man, why we never got hold of this one before totally baffles me. I mean totally. 21 bleedin' years, Brian. I mean, how come? How come we never got a whiff of this in 21 years?"

The reason, of course, why no-one got a whiff of this in all that time is basically because no-one wanted to talk about it. Not the parents. Not the doctors. Not the nurses. Certainly not the relatives. And not the friends because there haven't been any friends.

It is surprising, however, when you think what you do see on television these days and what you do read about in papers and, especially, in magazines. But, even today, this story has been released to a handful of people only. BBC2 has the exclusive. They alone, it is believed, will bring to the subject the seriousness and dignity it most certainly warrants. It is, after all, a very sensitive issue as the miniscule production team assigned to it is the first to admit. (Well, they would, when you think about it, wouldn't they?)

But as Hector, reporter, director and producer, keeps pointing out to Brian, cameraman and sound engineer (a) it is surprising that this is the first any of the media has heard of it and (b) it is quite staggeringly exciting as a piece of news. Yes, it will go down in the history books, if all goes well, alongside ... hard to say what exactly but it will feature as one of the GIANT STEPS FORWARD IN SURGERY at least. It is one of those "it's never been done before stories" after all. So let's hope it's going to work.

"I hope it's going to work," wishes Brian who immediately wishes he'd wished nothing of the kind out loud.

"Jesus Christ, Brian. Even if it doesn't bloody work we'll be the only ones to witness it, O.K. And, and think about this, Brian, think about this ... what are we going to see? I mean, what does it look like? What will it sound like? How has it survived, Brian, for 21 years, Brian, being what it is, Brian? I mean, Brian, what we're talking about here is a head, Brian. A head. We're talking, well, science fiction almost, Brian."

"We're talking horror movie, here, if you ask me, Hector."

Hector's out of his chair and on top of Brian in an instant. He has a hand clamped over Brian's mouth.

"Never, never, never let me hear that kind of language again. Never. We're here to do a serious piece of reporting about a very serious event which, face it, Brian, could change the course of history, could change the lives of, of, of, well ... quite a few ... and could provide hope for, for, for, well ... some ... anyway, enough, O.K. Shut up. Oh, oh, here he comes now," says Hector, clambering back into his seat.

The "he" is Albert Thomsen himself, a self-made man if ever there was one. Dragged himself up by his bootstraps he did, as he's more than happy to tell you and everyone else at every available opportunity. He was a Boy of Ambition who grew into a Man of Ambition, spurred on by a phenomenally boring marriage and a quite remarkable offspring, the birth of which occurred 21 years ago to the day.

"Mr.Thomsen, I'm Hector Hampshire, BBC, and this is Brian."

"No time for that here. Come, we'll do it in the car." Albert Thomsen is perspiring freely, a grin keeps throwing itself back and forth across his face and his eyes are pigwild with excitement. He can barely contain himself. It is, without doubt, a big day for Albert. "Follow me," he commands.

They follow him out to his spanking new Bentley. And, frankly, they don't like it. Hector likes to be in charge and he isn't. Brian doesn't like many things.

"Mr Thomsen, where .... "

"Call me Al."

"Mr Thomsen, Al, where would you like to begin?" asks Hector from the front passenger seat while Brian struggles in the back with problems of focus and exposure.

"How about at the beginning?" says Thomsen with a kind of naiveté. It's the kind of smart-ass, self-made manner he's famous for. Fuming, Hector realises there's nothing he can argue with.

"Very well then, it was, I believe, correct me if I'm wrong, the maternity wing of St. Luke's, yes? At precisely 5.25 pm when ... well ..." Hector's suddenly lost for words. For the first time ever he freezes, his mind blurs, he cannot think. Brian, sensing panic, quickly focusses on Thomsen.

Thomsen is quite unaware of the inner turmoil happening to the man beside him. "What a birth! Yes! It cannot be denied. Indeed not." Thomsen wipes his brow with a chamois leather which he's taken from the glove compartment. "Beryl, that's Mrs. Thomsen, you understand, had been in labour for some thirty hours or so and refused any inducement. First time's always the worst time, I always say. Don't you agree, Hector?" Thomsen grins lasciviously and grabs Hector's thigh.

Hector almost faints, gagging on a frantic intake of air.

"To continue," continues Thomsen, "I was doing what was expected of me at the time. I was pacing the waiting room floor, carpetless it was, with a flask filled with my own little concoction: fifths of advocaat, lemonade, vodka, Pimm's No.6 and angostura bitters. Delicious. Kept me going, let me tell you."

"I bet it did, Al. I bet it did." Hector is horrified. Brian keeps the camera on Thomsen.

"Yes. And suddenly at precisely 5.25, as you said, Hector, as you said, done a bit of homework I see, at 5.25 the door to the Maternity Ward bursts open. Nurses come dashing out, dashing! They're ripping off their masks, tugging at cords, holding onto caps, wrenching velcro, white as a sheet to a woman, speechless with terror. This one sister stops, sees me, eyes popping out of her face, shakes her head and is overcome with hysteria. Has to be led away. Tell you, couldn't tell whether she was laughing or crying. Made no difference. Hideous sound."

"What on earth did you do, Al? What was passing through your mind exactly at the time? Tell us, Al, in your own words." Hector's television sincerity is insufferable at times, even for Brian. He keeps the camera steadfastly on Thomsen.

"Whose words did you think I might use, Hector? Eh, ma boy? Frightened that you might be putting words in my mouth, lad? Have no fear." And with that he grabs Hector's thigh once more.

"yyyykkkk!" stifles Hector.

Meanwhile, they have travelled a mere mile and a half in the monstrous afternoon rush hour traffic which nowadays begins at around 2.30 and ends somewhere near 8.00.

"What did I do? I did the only sensible thing I could do, Hector me boy. I held my ground outside that door and drained my flask.

"Then this young whippersnapper of a doctor appears. He looks shell-shocked to me but he manages a smile, more of a smirk really, and tells me I must be brave, to prepare myself for a surprise and be ready to support Beryl through what was indeed going to be a very difficult time. Bernstein was his name. Remember that, it's important.

" 'What's up Doc?' I ask, you know the phrase I take it. 'What is it? Boy or a girl, eh, Doc? You can tell me, I'm the proud father.' I'm coming out with all this and, well, I think the contents of the flask were doing most of the talking, to be honest ... my legs felt a little weak, I have to say.

"And this little doctor just stands there with this funny look on his face and says something to the effect that it's more complicated than that. Yes, 'more complicated than that' were the words he used. 21 years and I can remember as if it were yesterday.

"Then he hits me with the real news. It's not so much a matter of whether Beryl's given birth to a boy or a girl, it's well .. the fact is it's a head. A living, breathing, smiling, eating, drinking, you name it, HEAD! How about that!!! And it's male, he believes. And male it turned out to be. Or we're the parents of the first bearded lady head, on the days when we forget to shave him.

"For once in my life, Hector, I was at a loss for words. Wouldn't you be? Wouldn't anyone? I was. So I walk past him and in to see Beryl who is so heavily sedated she didn't know who she was let alone what it was lying beside her on the bed. I mean I can talk about it now. Well, so I should be able to, 21 years later. But when Doc Bernstein told me, I didn't think I could take it, you know. And Beryl, Beryl was under sedation for weeks, months ... sometimes, between you and me, I think she still is, to this day. Oooops, the camera. We'll have to do a bit of editing, eh, lads? "

"Don't worry, Al, we'll be editing O.K."

"And as for the .. Head ... well, who'd have thought ..? I mean, it is a miracle."

"You could say that, Al, yes, you could," says Hector, regaining a little of his reporter's objectivity.

"And the miracle continues. That's another miracle." With this statement, Thomsen veers out across into the oncoming traffic and floors the accelerator.

"Jesus, Al," squeals Hector.

"Jesus, Al." echoes Brian.

"Miracles never cease," says Thomsen, calmly pulling back into the correct lane and turning off down a side street to his home.

"So.... So, Al, you got this call from Bernstein this morning?" Hector wishes the whole thing were over. He felt privileged to have been singled out for this very exclusive assignment. Now he questions the motives behind it.

"Always said he would call, Hector. Right from that day 21 years ago, he said he would call when the opportunity arose. And, Thomsen looks at his diver's Rolex, one hour and seventeen minutes ago, he made that call."

"Before we get on to that, Al..."

"Can you believe it, Hector, today of all days?" Thomsen breaks out into another mucksweat and dabs his forehead with the chamois leather.

"I can hardly believe any of it, Al. But that aside, tell us, do, before we go any further, tell us what's its ... his ... your ... his name, your ... "

"Our Head, Hector. Say it. After 21 years you can say it, Hector, believe me. His name is Jack. Jack, Hector. Plain simple Jack. Nothing fancy. Just something plain. A fine name for a fine head. A fine, honest, trustworthy, no bloody nonsense name for a head who's 21 Today. And what a present we have for him, eh? The Perfect Gift."

"Yes, to get back to that, Al. Could you tell us and the audience what Doctor Bernstein said when he called you today? I know we don't have much time, but please, if you would ..." Hector excels himself with this mind-numbing mixture of condescension and fawning.

"The first thing he said was 'How's Jack?' and I told him that Jack was fine, thankyou. He asked about his mental health and I asked him if he was joking. I mean what other health has a head, for God's sake, eh? He didn't think that was funny. A serious man. Jewish, of course. And brilliant. Totally brilliant.

"Well, cutting it short ... you know what had happened. But, for the camera, here it is: It appears, well, it more than appears, there was this most horrendous accident this morning right smack outside Bernstein's hospital. You know he has his own private hospital, the Moses Bernstein Memorial, dedicated to the memory of his mother, Marigold. I digress, forgive me. This accident. What a terrible thing. This young man in a sports car drives into an ambulance (surprised really that it doesn't happen more often, the way those ambulance drivers drive) and, anyway, he's killed outright. Not only killed, though .... he's ... wait for it ... he's been .... he's been bloody well decapitated ... AND ... not only that. He's Jack's age. AND NOT ONLY THAT." Thomsen is sweating profusely and driving in fits and starts so that Brian is having the Devil's own job trying to keep him in picture without too much flare from his forehead. "WAIT FOR THIS ... Bernstein tells me ... wait!... he tells me he can use the kid's body. The body is UNSCATHED, in perfect health, a perfect specimen to GUESS WHAT!!!!"

"Tell us, Al, tell us," says a calm, cool, calculating and oh-so earnestly involved Hector.

Thomsen picks up on Hector's calmness and tries to calm himself. "Bernstein says he can, Bernstein says he definitely can put Jack on top of the dead kid's body. He's got permission from the kid's parents, for Christ's sake, and everyone else. And, bugger me, oooops! Sorry, but you must understand what this means to me. And to Beryl and to Jack, of course. Bernstein foresees no problem. What a surprise for Jack, eh!"

"Indeed, yes. And, viewers, we are privileged and proud to be invited to witness the scene when, after 21 years of horizontal living, young Jack is offered a view of things he has never had before. From on top of a pair of strong young shoulders, from atop a body of a young man who, you could say, gave his own head that this .. that Jack might have the chance to live an upright and doubtless honest life."

Hector's delivery is masterful, as is his timing. He has let Thomsen take the floor, as it were, all the way up to now. Now the tension must build for the programme to work as theatre, as television. Hector has set the scene for that tension, it is built, it just has to be allowed to carry itself by its own momentum to the climax by the bed of Jack.

Thomsen is visibly moved by Hector's speech. He stares mistily into the lens, "What a birthday gift," he throatily whispers.

"Who could have imagined? Who could have chosen a more perfect way to thank 21 years of patience and goodness on the part of a young ..."

"That was going to be my line, Hector," says Thomsen, distraught suddenly. Robbed of his speech.

"It will be," reassures Hector remembering the marvels of television and editing, "it will be, by the bedside."

"Oh, thanks, Hector, thanks a million," says Thomsen, happy again, as he swings the Bentley into the driveway of his enormous Mock Tudor residence. For it is a "residence", most certainly it is.

Hector turns to camera as Brian refocusses, "Well, ladies and gentlemen, yes. Yes, here we are. On this historic occasion. Never, never, never has such a thing happened. Never on television. Never on anything. Never for real. Never before." He's lowered his voice about six octaves as if entering a cathedral while High Mass is taking place. Another Hector masterstroke. Pure television. "And now, now we are about to enter the Thomsen residence where the ... where Jack... unknowingly awaits ... unwittingly about to receive a 21st birthday present he will remember for the rest of his life. A gift none of us will forget, ladies and gentlemen. Least of all, Jack. The ul .. tim .. ate ... gift. But come, we must be quick."

Thomsen's already out of the car, his key in the lock of his front door.

Hector turns to his cameraman and sound engineer. This is Hector director/producer speaking: "Come on Brian, for crying out loud. This is the Big Moment. Next to the success or failure of Bernstein in the operating theatre, THIS IS IT. THE GIVING OF THE GIFT! This is the HUMAN PART!"

They catch up with Thomsen as he's saying a quick hello to the astonished Beryl. It occurs to both Hector and Brian that, first, Beryl knows nothing and, second, she's almost valiumed out of existence anyway.

Together the three men dash up the stairs and crash into one of the five bedrooms on the first floor. In the corner of the room is a cot, above which is suspended an angled mirror which displays a television image from a set positioned quite close to the cot. Thomsen switches off the set as they enter.

" 'ere, what the !!?" comes a very rough, very aggressive voice from the cot. It shakes Hector. What also shakes him a little is the absence of any other furniture in the room. Of course, he thinks, what need is there for chests of drawers, of wardrobes? What would be in them? What he does notice, however, is a stack of maybe twenty or so round cardboard boxes, one on top of the other in a corner of the room.

"Jack, Jack, Jack my boy ... it's your father." Thomsen speaks warmly, almost affectionately, but he cannot hide his excitement. He stands looking down into the cot. Hector and Brian join him. "And, Jack, this is Hector and this, or rather that, behind the camera is Brian. They're from television, Jack"

"Oh," says Jack as Hector, Brian and the wide world of TV get their first glimpse of what is, in truth, a very ordinary, rather plain-looking head of a white, male Caucasian who looks a trifle young for his admitted age of 21. "Why?" says Jack.

"Why, Jack? Why? I'll tell you why, Jack. I'll tell you why, sonny boy," Thomsen is rocking the cot in his excitement and has to be restrained by Brian who says his shot of Jack is not being improved by the fact that he keeps getting rolled about in the bed.

"Tell us all, Al, do. For this is the moment, Al, we have all been waiting for. Not least of all ..." says Hector as a voice-over part.

"Jack. Jack. It's your 21st Birthday. And Jack, have I got a present for you ..." Thomsen pauses to make the moment appropriately weighty for television.

Jack quickly glances over at the boxes in the corner of the room. He looks back at his father in abject horror.

"Oh, no Dad. Oh no. Not ... not another bloody hat!!!!!"
".............."

The silence is broken by Beryl's quietly pitiful voice calling from down the stairs. "An ambulance is here at the front door," she says. "It isn't for me, is it?"

"CUT!" cries Hector with tears coursing down his cheeks, though whether from anguish or joy no-one can tell.

LIES, LIES, LIES.
(or The Parrot with No Name.)

Can't abide lies. Can't be doing with them. As a humanitarian and animal lover and trainer/manager of macaws, budgerigars, paralettes, parakeets and parrots for more years than I prefer to recall, I tell you I cannot stand deception. Always believed in the truth. Always will. Cost me dearly over the years. Cost me friendships. Cost me money. Cost me a wife. Cost me the life of a poodle we owned. True. I told the truth to the detective. Yes, I said, it was Bertie who bit the bugger. Yes, my dear, sweet 17 year old miniature poodle did bite the brute who spat at my friend Dolly (for no reason whatsoever, I might add). Yes he did. So what did they do about it? They took Bertie away and they put him to sleep. Said it was the only thing they could do, under the circumstances. The wages of truth, eh? The price you pay for being honest.

But you didn't come here to hear about Bertie. You want the real story behind the famous Parrot with No Name, right? Well, having come all the way to my villa here in Marbella, you deserve more than the story. Be my guest for a few days. No really, I insist. Plenty of room, really. Enjoy yourself, that's what this place is here for.

Anyway, while you're making up your mind, I'll tell you what happened. I first came upon him in Fulham. Oh yes, I should make one other thing clear. Along with lies, I cannot stand to see birds caged up. Better caged than beer-battered and deep-fried I suppose, however. However, I was passing this vicar's house at the time when this voice booms out, "WANKER!". Now one other thing you should realise is that I've had it with soccer hooliganism. Drives me to distraction. Never happened in my day. Why today? I don't know. Affluence. I put it down to that and the fact there's no National Service, I suppose. That's it if you want my opinion.

Discipline. That's what's missing today.

Which brings me back to the shout I heard from the Vicarage. Well, you could have knocked me down with a feather. Hearing that kind of language. Hearing the kind of obscenity you might well expect these days on the terraces of Anfield or Highbury coming from a Vicarage, for God's sake. Really. So, up the front path I go and bang on the door. And this little vicar opens it. Felt sorry for the bugger I did. Poor little sod.

"I'm sorry," says he.

"No, I'm sorry," says I.

"It's that bird."

"What bird?"

"Bird in the window," says he.

And there it is, the monster, the football hooligan. A fully-fledged parrot the size of a young German Shepherd. And caged up. That did it. The cage. Couldn't stand to look at the swine in that cage. I mean a bastard he is all right with a mouth like that. But to cage him up is criminal.

"You're a criminal," I said to the vicar.

"You know me?" says he, white as his dog collar.

"What you talking about?"

"All those years ago," he says, "before ..." There's no blood left in him.

"What you talking about?" I repeat.

"Porridge. Doin' time," says he, eyes suddenly lost-looking, you know. "I thought everyone would have forgotten by now."

"Forget it," says I, cottoning on at last. "I want that parrot."

"He's yours!" says he, almost before I'd finished the sentence.

Weeks later, now, having cleansed the beast's mouth by every means I could lay my hands on, using everything from carbolic soap to threats of sound thrashings, I found myself in a bit of a predicament. Here was a bird who liked to talk.

Talk, talk, talk, talk. Night and day, day and night. Never stopped. Everything he saw, he commented on. And I was living, remember, in a tiny bedsit in Fulham at the time. So he saw a lot. He saw everything. And he used to make wise-cracks when girls came around. And when they stayed. It was very embarrassing for all concerned at times, I tell you. But I really didn't care. My wife had divorced me and taken every-thing. And I didn't care about these girls. They were out for as much of a good time as I was. Nothing more, nothing less.

Then, as I said, it happened. I fell in love. No, really. And there was he in the corner of my one room, ready, willing and able to destroy this wonderful relationship just by opening his mouth and saying something crass, or worse, in front of Betsy, my beloved Betsy. So I thought it over and decided it was for the best to tell the parrot the truth and ask for his assistance, as a friend. Well, bugger me. I should have known better.

I had arranged for Betsy to come round to my place on this Friday. So Thursday night I take the parrot to one side, as it were, and I tell him.

"Listen, you," I say, "this is serious now."

"Since when have you ever been serious?" says he.

"Since I met Betsy."

"What? WHAT?!!!!"

"I'm serious."

"Aw, come off it," says the parrot and starts to turn quite nasty.

"Listen to me," I say, very firmly, "tomorrow night Betsy is coming round here."

"Terrific! Something new. Wonderful!" says he, with a really dirty look in his beady eye.

"You missed my point. She's coming here because she loves me and I love her. It's not just sex."

"WHAAAT!!!!!????" he screeches.

"No. No, no, no."

"You must be bloody JOKING!" says he with a most unpleasant smirk. That did it.

"Get this into your thick head and into your horrible little mind. Tomorrow evening, when Betsy comes here, you face the corner of the room. And if you so much as turn your head and even try to take a peek, even try, mind you, or you say one one ... one word, I mean it .... I'll ...."

"You'll what?" asks he, a little subdued. He finally can see I'm in no mood for jokes.

"One look, one word ..." I really spell it out now, "and it's back to the zoo you go.

Me, who's so against caging up birds or any creatures. Can you imagine me saying this? But I was mad, I tell you. This was serious. I had to make it clear and lay it on the line.

"I don't believe this," says the parrot, more to himself than to anyone else. He believed it, all right. Oh yes, he believed it.

"Better believe it," I said. "One look, one word and ... back to the zoo you go."

Well, the following night, I bring home Betsy and there he is, glaring at us as we walk in the door.

"Evening," says I.

"Evening, Miss," says he in his nicest voice. Then he looks at me with an expression he's clearly been practising. It is supposed to say that he doesn't give a damn, he's going to miss nothing and see if he cares. Which I suppose, to some degree, it does. Then he turns to the corner of the room. It is a most pleasant surprise, I can tell you.

Anyway, to say the very least, Betsy and I have a whale of a time. She really was a wonderful girl. We quite forgot the parrot. He didn't try to look round and he stayed very quiet. It really was as if he wasn't there. It was terrific, really. And what a change from those other nights when I'd seen and heard him join in with advice, criticism, encouragement and often with laughter and whistling.

We had such a marvellous time, Betsy and I, that she

suggests we make a weekend of it and go stay at some country inn she knows out in Berkshire. Well, why not? Sounds a great idea to me. So I suggest she throws a few things into my smallest suitcase (my ex-wife had left sweaters and things, so I told Betsy to help herself). Meanwhile I made a few phone calls. When I'm done, I see she has everything packed including my silk dressing gown which is on top of everything in the case. It's causing a problem. Every time she closes the lid, a bit of it slides out.

"It keeps slipping out. There must be a way around this," she says to me, a little out of breath.

The parrot shifts uneasily on his perch. It's the first move I've seen him make all evening.

"Look," I suggest, "why don't you sit on it while I try to push it in."

The parrot shifts again.

"It's not working, darling," says Betsy, now quite flushed. "You're going to have to sit on it and I'll try and push it in."

We try it. The parrot shifts again. We're both rather pink in the face and there's quite a lot of puffing and panting going on by this stage.

"It's still not working, Betsy. I know! Let's both sit on it and both try to push it in."

At this, the parrot literally does a complete about face in one hop and screeches out, "Zoo or no zoo, this I have to see!"

Betsy lets out this incredible guffaw and we both topple to the floor in hysterical laughter.

What a character! I mean, you've got to hand it to him. And, on top of everything, now that he's cured of really bad swearing, he couldn't fail. His reputation had already spread fairly far but this incident, so often recounted not only by myself but by Betsy (who's in P.R., for heaven's sake), really made him famous. He was, as they say in showbiz, "on his way".

The thing that did it, of course, was the tragedy of the plumber. Well, I saw it as a tragedy. Still do. But old Mrs

Fitzpatrick loved to tell that story. I can still hear her laughter. Dreadful old bitch.

By this time, we were living, the parrot and I, in a terrace house off Fulham Broadway. Very pleasant. Very overpriced. Very chic. Or so the estate Agents would have you believe. And "on the way up" like, you could say, the occupants.

Mrs Fitzpatrick lived next door. She was paralysed from the neck down so she didn't get out much. Her daughter looked after her when she wasn't at work. Which she was most days from 7 in the morning till 9 at night. God knows what she did. Dear God also knows what Mrs Fitzpatrick did, for that matter. Not a lot, I surmise. Except listen. She was a great listener. And she was the one who heard what happened.

I had a problem with the kitchen sink and I'd called the plumber who said he could come the following morning and take a look at the pipes. I explain that I have to leave the house early that morning so I will leave the front door unlocked. He said that would be fine and I promptly forgot all about it.

As promised, the plumber turns up at the house the following morning. And he finds the door is locked so he bangs on the door and rings the bell. The parrot hears this and in his finest imitation of Lucy of "I Love Lucy" (which he did) fame shouts out, "Who is it?"

The plumber replies, "It's the plumber, I've come to mend the pipes."

"Who is it?" shouts Lucille Ball (who, unfortunately, was not one of the plumber's TV favourites so she went unrecognised).

"It's the plumber. I've come to mend the pipes," shouts the plumber.

"Who is it?" shouts Lucy.

"IT'S THE PLUMBER. I'VE ...COME... TO... MEND... THE... PIPES!"

And so it continues on and on. And, believe it or not, the plumber ends up having a heart attack right there on the doorstep and dies.

Well, totally ignorant of this whole episode, I get home late that night. It was dark, I remember, as I fumbled with the key in the lock. Next thing, I'm tripping over something quite bulky as I enter the house.

"Who is it?" I wonder quite instinctively. It's a kind of reflex action, something you just shout out.

"It's the plumber," says the parrot. "He's come to mend the pipes."

"Why do you sound like somebody I should recog ..?" I never completed the question. Mrs Fitzpatrick let out this salvo of snorts which culminate in a screech of laughter worthy of a flock of parrots the size of B52s. We heard her through the wall like she was sitting beside us. The whole street heard her. Most of Fulham heard her, in fact. And that was it. The story was out. And of course, the television people arrived, newspaper reporters, everyone. And, in no time, he was famous. As famous as Lucille Ball. More famous, in truth, in England for a time.

That was when the trouble began. You see, he realised what had made him a star. A one-liner. He wanted more. And he began making things up. Ask him a simple qustion and you never knew what he might reply. Certainly not the truth if he could think of something funny to say.

One day, you'd get reporters asking him his name. Well, he would be as likely to say Mel Blanc as Chips Rafferty. The next day, he'd tell people his name was Pretty Boy or Skipper. Then he would call himself The Duke or Firestone Hammer III of Wordbridge and concoct some monstrous pedigree as long as your arm. Basically, he developed into a very untrustworthy and totally egocentric piece of work. A right royal pain in the arse, basically. And a nameless one at that, in truth.

So, to cut the story short, I flogged him to a property developer who'd just bought a chain of pubs from a nearby brewery that had gone bust. Didn't get that much for him, either, though I heard he thinks I did. No, his reputation for lying had spread as fast as his reputation for humour. I mean, when you can't tell when somebody is being funny and when they're not, it can get a bit tricky. And, by this time, you could not believe a word he said.

With the proceeds of the sale, by the way, I bought a dog. A big black mongrel who, incidentally, loved vodka and tonic and just loved to talk, too. A very interesting animal, all in all. But, sadly, I had to get rid of him after I'd made robbing banks my career and, following a chain of spectacular successes right through the 70's and early 80's, retired out here to Spain to take it easy and simply enjoy what's left of my life.

As for the parrot, well, I believe he became a bit of an old misery who hates jokes. Still tells tales. All lies, of course. Oh yes. All lies. But in a pub, who cares any way? Apart from a few people like myself. Can't abide lies, you know ...

THE FAN

"The nerve of the fellow, the nerve of the man. Shouting like that. How could he think of doing such a thing? How could he know? How could he even begin to guess? Did he think he might even come close? With so many names: American names, so many French, English, Scottish, so many, so many Serbian, Hungarian, Italian, Latvian, Irish, Gambian, Welsh, Nigerian, Argentinian, Peruvian, Libyan, Spanish, so many names, let alone the number of Polish names.

Here in a crowd of how many? Of 70,000? 90,000? 80,000? Shouting like that, shouting over the roar of such a crowd as this. Calling out that way. And why? Could he not have waited? At least, until a break in the play. At least until the Quarter was over, until Half-Time. Yes, better, Half-Time. But no, not him. The impatience of the man. The impudence of the man. Shouting like that. Disgusting, I call it.

I have heard of nothing like this before. Never. No. Nothing like it back home in my native Gdansk. No, nothing in my native Poland. Not on my travels, either. Not since leaving my homeland. Thinking back. No. But I reminisce. I have been here in America what, four years maybe? Yes. Four years, yes. And no, nothing. And, yes, I cannot help thinking back.

I cannot help thinking, thinking of the past. But enough of that. What point is there, to that? To family, to friends missed. What point is there to that now?

Perhaps it is a joke, yes. An American joke. Perhaps yes. Perhaps I miss the point. Perhaps a racial joke. They like jokes, I know they do. They like their jokes like they like their football sometimes. Sometimes with a passion, sometimes dispassionate. They like jokes tough, hard, dirty, yes. Hurtful, harmful, cold, hot, angry, painful, yes. And cruel, often cruel. Sometimes not for the fun of it at all. So it seems to me. Sometimes, yes, though. Yes, for the fun. I must be fair. Oh, yes, I laugh, too. I laugh, yes, sometimes.

But calling out a name like that, at random. Where is the joke in that? At such a time? See, I love this game. I love football more than anything. Like most of these fans do. Like any fan. What is the harm in that? I love my Giants, my team. I hate all other teams, yes. Hate them. Hate is not too strong a word. But no, I am not stupid. I know they must exist, of course, yes. Where would we be without them? There would be no game, of course. Without other teams, where would the game be? That is funny. That is a joke, yes. But I am not laughing. I am confused still and angry, yes.

Yes, I am angry with the man. He is a man like myself.

A fan, a fanatic like myself, maybe as far from the land of his birth as I, maybe, as new to the excitement and thrill of it all as I, yes. But no. Impossible. Most definitely. No, no, no, no, no. Not a fan like me, no, not shouting like that when such a play was going on here before us in the Second Quarter of this game with my Giants coming back, storming back, I should say, storming, my Super Heroes of last year's Super Bowl, yes. Once more to take it again this year, this year, next year, and so on and so forth. Yes, oh yes. And ... and what does this fellow do?

He shouts a name.

'Steve.'

'Stevo!'

'STEVE!'

'STEVE!'

'STE-VE!!!!!!!!!!'

He shouts and shouts and shouts. Over the roar of the crowd. Over the voices of fans cheering and cheering. Over the voices of hundreds and thousands of fans like myself who have come here to watch the game and see my Giants win. Yes, win, win win win.

How dare a man do this? Even here in America? Even here in America with its freedoms? Here in this stadium? He is no fan. I have to see who this man is. I must know, I must respond. I stand and turn and look when he calls, looking back, missing the play action, yes, and all I can see is a sea of people, of fans roaring and shouting.

Does he know me? No, he does not know me. Oh, yes, he may have seen me before. Seen me here before. Oh, many, many times. Then he must know I am a fan. A great fan. One of the greatest Giants' fans. A Giant-sized fan. A Giant of a Fan. Oh, yes. But he does not know me. How could he know my name? Me, an immigrant. From a country where names are ..... are what? Different? Well, no. Not really. Are used differently? No, not at all. Are what then? Hard to say. Yes. Hard to pronounce unless you are Polish, of course. But I am no longer Polish. Yes, I am from Poland. I am a Pole. But I am American.

Oh, yes, I am sometimes, as you say, the butt of a joke. Often unkind, yes. But then, if it is humorous, then I laugh. I laugh with anyone. With everyone. When it is funny.

'Steve.'

'Steve!'

'STEVE!'

'STEVE!'.

'STE-VE!!!!!!!!!!!'

He shouted and shouted. And, yes, I had to tell him. I had to explain. I a foreigner. But I am a citizen of this great country. And my name is no longer my given name. It is no longer my Saint's birthday name. It is my new given name. I had to explain. I had to tell the man.

And who am I here in Giants Stadium on this November Sunday afternoon? Who am I? I am a Giant of a fan whose name is not Steve!!, is not STEVE!!, is not STEVE!! no matter how loud he calls it. My name, this Sunday afternoon is, I will tell you what it is.

It is Raul Allegre Ottis Anderson Bill Ard Carl Banks Mark Bavaro Brad Benson Jim Burt Harry Carson Maurice Carthon Mark Collins Eric Dorsey Tony Galbreath Chris Godfrey Andy Headen Kenny Hill Jeff Hostetler Byron Hunt Bob Johnson

Damian Johnson Thomas Johnson Brian Johnston Robbie Jones
Terry Kinard Sean Landeta Greg Lasker Leonard Marshall
George Martin Phil McConkey Solomon Miller Joe Morris
Zeke Mowatt Karl Nelson Bart Oates Elvis Patterson Gary
Reasons William Roberts Stacy Robinson Lee Rouson Jeff
Rutledge Jerome Sally Phil Simms Lawrence Taylor Vince
Warren John Washington Herb Welch Perry Williams Bill
Parcells.

That is my name in America. In Giants Stadium. And if
ever I should discover who it was who shouted 'Steve' in the
middle of an important play like that, you know what I will do?
This Giant will crush that man. I say CRUSH that man. But
wait, they're coming out for the Second Half. Do you hear the
roar of the fans? Hear it. You hear that? Hear those voices.
Fans' voices. Voices of real fans. Fans like me, like me."

* * * *

When asked on the journey home, stuck in traffic after the
game, what the big fellow had been muttering about throughout
Half-Time, Joey Thomas of Queens had this to say, "Did you
see him? Did you seen all those Giants badges, his scarf, his
hat? Did you see his face, painted red, white and blue? Did you
see him? Boy, does he support the Giants, or what?

"What the hell he was on about I dunno, though. He was
foreign. Oh sure, he was foreign. Sounded, I dunno, maybe
Russian. I dunno. What do I know? All I know is that we
were moving up fast and we was on their 20 yard line on a
fourth and two and things were pretty tense and it looked like
we were beginning to play like SuperBowl Champs after all and
Phil had the ball and was looking for Mark and it all went a bit
quiet and I heard this incredible scream from behind us.

"Steve! STEVE! STEVE!!!!" this guy was shouting at the
top of his lungs and I look at our man sitting next to me, the
Ruskie or whatever, who like me's just tryin' to watch the
game. And he's up, standing up and turning round. And the
shout goes up again. And he's up again and turning round,

looking. And he looks pretty wild, you know. And he sits down. And it happens again and again and there's fumble after fumble after we got our First. And it's getting real tense now. "And it happens again. 'STEVE!!' this guy way up behind us shouts again. And our man looks at me real quick, like he's shocked, surprised, even scared a little. But real wild. And he leaps up and turns round and shouts at the top of his voice, in that accent of his, he shouts, 'MY NAME'S NOT STEVE!!!" and with that, he sits down again."

"He was probably Polish," says Tom, Joey's elder brother, who's driving and who, in his time, has been known both to play football and tell jokes.

"HAVE YOU HEARD ABOUT..... ?"

These three stories were being told in London advertising circles before I left in 1983. I take no credit whatsoever for their marvellous invention, merely for remembering them. The interesting thing is that they were told about real people. Two were told as serious, true stories (up until the punchline). They aren't too nice, either. But the nice thing about them is that you can tell them yourself and change the names to any names you wish. What are enemies for, if not to tell nasty stories about? Here, I confess, I've changed the real names to protect the guilty just as much as the innocent.

The first tale concerns the four principals of an advertising agency we shall call Man, MacMillan, Ashcroft and Welsh. Four quite brilliant men who were regarded by very many as being thoroughly objectionable people.

One morning the agency gets a call to visit a prospective new client and pitch their business. The four men leap into their company Mercedes and roar off to the meeting. So eager are they to get there before any other agency, they run a red light and WHAM they smash headlong into a truck. The car is a total write- off and so, indeed, are they.

The scene changes to the reception area in Hell. Man, MacMillan, Ashcroft and Welsh impatiently await the Devil. They're really pissed off, mainly for losing the opportunity to pitch and brilliantly win that piece of new business.

The Devil appears finally and asks which of the men is Man. Man slowly gets to his feet, showing no respect for the little chap with the pointy beard, horns and tail.

"Follow me," says the Devil and leads him off down a corridor. He then opens the first of a number of doors. Inside is a bedroom with, on the filthiest bed imaginable, the filthiest whore imaginable. She's covered in sores which ooze pus, she's rotting from within and without. The stench is incredible.

"Mr Man for being the most thoroughly objectionable person for most of your life, this is yours for Eternity."

With that, the Devil pushes the speechless-for-once Man into the room and slams and locks the door behind him.

Back goes the Devil to reception and calls for Welsh. Welsh follows him down the corridor past Man's door. The Devil opens the next door to reveal an equally horrendous woman in equally horrendous circumstances.

"Mr Welsh, for being the most thoroughly objectionable person for most of your life, this is yours for Eternity."

With which, the Devil pushes the horrified Welsh into the room and slams and locks the door behind him.

Back goes the Devil to reception and calls Ashcroft. Ashcroft follows him down the corridor, past Man's door, past Welsh's door, to the third door which the Devil opens. Inside, you guessed, is a similar scene to the first two. Ashcroft cannot believe his eyes and ears.

"Mr Ashcroft, for being the most thoroughly objectionable person for most of your life, this is yours for Eternity," says the Devil and pushes the stupefied Ashcroft into the room and slams and locks the door behind him.

"So..." says the Devil, back in reception, "you must be MacMillan." And they immediately get into an argument about that, MacMillan being the kind of person MacMillan is. But in the end, he owns up to being who he is and follows the Devil down the same corridor. They pass Man's door, Welsh's door and Ashcroft's door and the Devil then opens the fourth door.

There inside is the most exquisitely furnished bedroom you've ever seen. And there on the freshly-laundered cotton sheets is the freshly-showered, freshly-oiled and freshly-scented Bo Derek, stark and perfectly naked.

Then the Devil says, as he pushes the astonished MacMillan into the room, "Bo Derek, for being the most thoroughly objectionable....."

(Seriously, of course, it doesn't have to be Bo Derek. My apologies, Bo. Make it who you wish. It was really just kind of, well, inverted flattery. That's all.)

The second story is told about two middle-aged admen, long time rivals, who bump into each other after a long, long separation. They immediately get into a conversation about the business (what else?) and what they are doing in it.

Well, it transpires that one of them, let's call him Brugman, has just started up his own agency. The other, Lofthouse, is slightly miffed about this (something he's always threatened to do himself but never done, not having the necessary confidence or what-have-you) and needs to know all about it. Mainly, of course, who Brugman has got to join him in the venture, this being key to its success or failure.

"For a start," says Brugman, "I've got this terrific copywriter."

"What's his name?"

"Name's Brignull," says Brugman smugly.

"Not ... Not Tony Brignull?" asks a fascinated and slightly horrified Lofthouse who cannot believe for the life of him that Brugman could have pulled off such a coup.

"Er, well, no," says Brugman, "Tommy Brignull, actually. Very good man."

"Oh. Never heard of him," says Lofthouse, visibly relieved and reassured.

"And I've got this great art director. Name of Godfrey."

"Not Neil Godfrey!" cries the astonished Lofthouse: Neil being as good as they get.

"Er ... no," says Brugman. "Charlie. Yes Charlie Godfrey, actually."

"Oh," says Lofthouse. "Don't know the man."

"Very good."

"No doubt," doubts Lofthouse. "And who have you managed to get as your head of Account Services?"

"Man by the name of Mead," says Brugman, casually.

"Not Peter Mead?!!!? Don't tell me he's chucked in his own, massively successful agency to come and join you! Has he?"

"Er, no. No. Not Peter .... Sam Mead's his name."

"Oh. Oh. And who have you managed to get as your all-important Creative Director, eh?"

"Man by the name of Chapman, actually," says Brugman with a hint of reservation.

"Not Tony Chapman?!!!!?"

"Yes, Tony Chapman," says Brugman. "That's the man!"

Thirdly, we have the tale of an advertising agency art buyer. Let's call her Toni Chapman, shall we?

This is the background:

Toni runs her department with an iron fist in an iron glove. She treats everyone with equal contempt. Nobody is beneath it, especially not reps. To Toni, reps are the lowest of the low. They are mere messengers who make their money on other people's talent. And there is no way she will let a rep get past her to see an art director with the work of his photographer or illustrator until she has seen him first. Toni, naturally, being always too busy to see anyone.

To put it mildly, Toni is not loved by reps. Neither is she loved much by art directors who have called in the reps in the first place. However, this last point is sort of irrelevant except that the story, told as the truth, does hinge on this general lack of warmth and affection felt towards the woman.

The story goes as follows:

One Monday morning, a rep turns up at the reception desk of the massive ad agency where Toni works.

"Hello. I have a nine o'clock appointment with Toni Chapman," he says brightly, brimming with confidence.

"Oh, oh dear," says the receptionist who's somewhat flustered and not a little upset. "Yes, well, you couldn't have known but ... oh, this is terrible ... "

"What's the problem? I do have an appointment. Really," says the rep. He's run into this kind of tactic too many times to be in the slightest put out.

"Oh, I'm sure you do ... No, no. It's not that," says the receptionist. "It's well, it's just that ... on Friday night, driving home, Toni was involved in the worst car crash. She was crushed, trapped there in her car for hours and hours. Nobody could get near her, she was screaming and crying and bleeding profusely. What's so dreadful is that she remained conscious, suffering the most ghastly pain, right up until the end which didn't come until five on Saturday morning. Oh, it's too awful, too awful." The receptionist is terribly upset. She's imagining it happening to herself.

The rep stands there looking appropriately shocked and saddened. "I'm very sorry," he whispers solemnly and turns and leaves.

The following morning at the same time, however, the same rep appears at the same reception desk and tells the same receptionist that he has a nine o'clock appointment with the same Toni Chapman.

Now a lot of people come and go through a reception area of an agency this big. A lot of the same people do so a lot of times. And the receptionist doesn't think twice about this. She recognises the man vaguely as she vaguely recognises a number of people.

"I'm sorry," she says, "You obviously haven't heard."

"Heard what?" says the rep with a brilliant smile.

"About Toni."

"What about Toni?" he asks, holding that smile.

"About her most tragic accident, driving home last Friday. About how she suffered and died most frightfully."

"Why no," says the rep, losing the smile.

So the receptionist recounts the story for him once more and the rep, duly saddened, listens. When she's finished, he whispers solemnly, "I'm sorry" and turns and leaves.

Well, dammit all, if he doesn't show up again the following day. Same time, same place, same receptionist, same request to see the same Toni Chapman. This time the receptionist isn't sure about this. But she's not sure enough to ask him anything. I mean, what sort of man would ... No, nobody would do such a thing, would they?

So the whole rigamarole is acted out once again. The terrifying accident, the stupendous suffering, the nightmare death. And the saddened-looking rep whispers solemnly that he's sorry and turns and leaves.

But wait. Thursday morning arrives and at 8.55 a.m. would you believe this? Look who's standing here in the reception of the agency. Asking to see you know who. The receptionist is sure this time. Oh yes. She's certain. And she's cross.

"Forgive me," she demands crossly, "but aren't you the very same rep who was in here yesterday at this time asking to see Toni Chapman? And weren't you here the day before that and the day before that? And didn't I tell you all about the tragedy and the suffering that befell her?"

"Oh yes," says the rep with his most charming smile. "It's just that I love hearing the story."

Not nice? Well, no. Especially should you happen to hear it being told about you. A total fabrication and told as truth, too. However, I thought it funny. Let's hope that the real "Toni" did, along with the real "Tony" and the real Messrs Man, MacMillan, Ashcroft and Welsh of the other little tales.

Only a joke, fellas.

Really.

WHAT A LAUGH!

Would you believe, it all began with a small notice in the local parish magazine? What it said was the following:

A BIG NIGHT OF LAUGHS!
Sat. Aug. 12th.
Comedians, pranksters,
jokers of all kinds are
welcome. Pro. or Amat.
Old, young, male, female,
or bi. Licensed bar. Adm. 50p.
VILLAGE HALL,
DARLEY,
NORTH YORKS.

Innocuous as it first appeared, that notice got noticed. Not only locally in the parish. During the week leading up to the Big Night, word got out and travelled far and wide. Very far, very wide. And by Friday, there was even TV coverage. Cameras whirred outside the Hall as interviews with knowns and unknowns were conducted in a kind of prematch frenzy. There was an atmosphere of festival crossed with competition, of game, of sport, of fun, of fame, of fortune.

By Saturday, farmers' fields had been given over to hundreds, thousands of campers. Every hotel, pub, bed & breakfast joint, every place possible had been filled in an area approximately 20 miles square. There was talk of "Woodstock". There was all kinds of talk. There were questions, too.

How could the Village Hall hold such a crowd?

How could so many acts perform in the course of one single evening? Should it be made into a 3 Day Event?

How could it all go off without a hitch?

How had it all come about?

They were some of the questions most people asked. They were some of the questions no-one bothered to even try to answer. One question we all knew the answer to, however. That was this: How come so many people, not just from the United Kingdom now, mind you, but from Europe and America, had come?

They wanted laughter. They wanted to laugh. Or, alternatively, they wanted the other side of that coin. They wanted death. They wanted to see comics die, as they say. Or they wanted both. I believe, personally, that most wanted both. That's just my opinion.

The Big Night certainly got off to a flying start. Quite unannounced and quite unexpectedly, the Red Arrows showed up. This famous R.A.F. display team provided the opening number.

My, how exciting it was! Quite insane, of course. But quite awesome. Quite. The noise was deafening as those little red jets swooped low across the village rooftops and in and out the Hall, miraculously avoiding the rafters above, the crowds below and themselves in between. It was a truly staggering performance, unparalleled in the history of the Red Arrows and unrivalled by any aerobatic team anywhere in the world. We were most privileged to witness it.

Then came the acts. Dear Lord, were they awful! Jim and I hit the advertised Licensed Bar the moment we heard those creaky old one-liners like what's purple and weighs 27 tons? Moby Grape. Oh, no. Oh, dear. I mean, give us a break.

Unfortunately, you could still hear most of the acts even back here at the bar. But things did liven up. Ken Dodd, the famous comedian, phoned in with a joke which happens to be my favourite radio joke of all time.

"When I was very young, my parents were so poor they couldn't afford to buy me any clothes. So I couldn't go out. But when I was 14, they bought me a hat so I could look out of the window."

Jim and I were in hysterics, I tell you. So were many other people. And just then, in walked three tortoises of three very distinct ages. On their way, they said, to a Tortoise Rally and they'd dropped in for a beer since it was now raining outside and they'd forgotten to bring umbrellas. A likely story, but who's going to argue?

The old tortoise said he wasn't going to go back for the umbrellas because, he said, by the time he'd done that and got back he'd be too exhausted to continue on to the Rally. Fair enough?

The middle-aged tortoise said he wasn't going to go back for the umbrellas because, he said, by the time he'd done that and got back and had gone to the Rally, he'd be too exhausted to get home again. Fair enough?

The baby tortoise said quite categorically that he wasn't going to go back for the umbrellas because, he said, they would drink his beer. At which point, a shaggy dog walked up to their table and told them to cut it short because he'd been in a bar where something similar had occurred and it had taken years for them to get to the point. Some point, eh?

The old and middle-aged tortoises then give their solemn promise that if he goes they won't drink his beer. So, with some reluctance, he goes off out the door into what has become a most horrible night. It's thundering and lightning like a Wagnerian stage act.

It's then that Jim points out something very interesting. A comedian is dying telling the worst jokes imaginable like: You know a Jew was responsible for the sinking of the Titanic? Don't be stupid, it was an iceberg. Iceberg, Goldberg, what's the difference? What Jim has spotted is that factions are forming in the audience. All sorts of groups of people of the same career, mindset, profession, job, you name it, are getting together in groups. It's fascinating.

For example, just to go through a few I noticed instantly, there was a group of grandmothers, of Long John Silver impersonators, of cuckolds, of travelling salesmen, of landlords and their daughters, of whores with hearts of gold, of whores without them, of nuns, of vicars, of priests, of police and every arm of the armed forces, of plumbers, of builders, of saints, of sinners. Yes, it was odd. But then it was developing into that kind of night all round.

The jokes by now had moved, inevitably, into the ethnic arena with lots of anti-Black, anti-Polish and anti-Irish stories. Which causes some consternation in the audience, oddly, not among the Blacks, Poles and Irish I can see there but among other groups who take it upon themselves to defend other minorities (or majorities if the case arises) against such onslaughts.

A most bizarre alignment of sympathies has taken place as a result of two comedians (who, as it happens, die) telling an Irish and a Polish joke simultaneously.

The Irish joke involves the foreman on a building site shouting "Green side up, lads" to his workers which was a puzzlement to the teller until he saw that they were laying turf. The Polish joke involved a similar foreman on a building site calling Lech, or whoever, and asking him if he would go and get him a pack of Benson & Hedges and giving him the money to get the cigarettes. The Pole then, intelligently, asks what if they don't have any Benson & Hedges in the store. The foreman says he doesn't really care and says to the Pole to bring back anything he likes. So the Pole comes back with a ham sandwich.

Funny how allegiences form, isn't it? The nuns in the audience were the first to move, of all people, and some schoolteachers who got together with the landlords and their daughters and they "took out" the teller of the Irish joke. Meanwhile, used car salesmen, vicars, a few gladiators, the occasional P.R. person and sinners did the same for the Poles.

At which point in the proceedings, I hear the old tortoise bellow that the baby tortoise's beer is getting flat and that they ought to drink it. The middle-aged tortoise reminds him, mildly, that they've given their word and that a tortoise's word is its bond.

Then, would you believe, in walks this wonderful white horse. He comes straight up to the bar and orders himself a beer. The barman gives him one and, I suppose, as a gesture to make him feel a little more at home, he asks if the white horse knows that there's a famous Scottish whisky named after him.

The horse calmly looks at the barman and says, "What, Eric?"

He then drinks up, thanks the bewildered barman, and leaves.

The comedians onstage are having an exceptionally hard time in the ethnic arena which culminates in a particularly offensive racial conversation. "How," asks one standup comic "do you save a Pakki from drowning?" "I don't know," answers another. "Good!" says the first.

Up leap shopstewards, travelling salesmen, virgins, convicted thieves and mothers-in-law and the two comics, so-called, die a truly horrible death in full view of the entire audience.

Then a Marching Band from S.M.U. or P.D.Q.S. or B.V.D. or somewhere in the good old U.S.A. swing in through the doors and pull the party back together again. It's still pouring with rain outside, by the way. And I hear the old tortoise saying that the baby tortoise has probably been washed away and that his beer's getting very flat and that they should drink it. And the middle-aged tortoise has quite a job on his hands preventing the old fool from doing just that.

These comedians are really asking for trouble now. What posseses them to get up there in the first place beats me. But to then attack your audience seems like sheer suicide. After a particularly cheap Scottish homosexual joke involving two characters by the names of, would you believe, Ben Doon and Phil McCavity, this woman starts on a Long John Silver story and, to everyone's surprise, it's a cracker. It's about two actors who meet. Both have been out of work for some time and one has finally landed a part and it's a big one. He's going to play Long John Silver and it pays an astounding £2,000 a week. The other actor can hardly believe his ears. Why, he wants to know, given that, is he waiting until next week to start? Why isn't he starting now? Well, says John, he's decided to go in for realism this time and he's having a leg off for the part and it will take a day or two for him to become acclimatised to a wooden stump. The other actor thinks he's taking it all a bit seriously but he does see John's point. £2,000 a week parts don't happen every day and it would be a shame to lose it for the sake of a leg (if losing a leg could save it).

Anyway, a month or so goes by and they happen to bump into each other again and now not only has John got a wooden leg. He also has an eye patch and a hook for a hand. Seeing this, the other actor expresses alarm that John should have decided to go so far in the name of realism. A part being only a part, after all. John explains it wasn't quite like that, at all. No, what happened was that on his day off, he'd decided to go deep sea fishing. During the course of which, he gets a line caught around his wrist and it literally whipped off his hand.

"What about your eye, though?" asks the other actor.

"Even easier to explain," says John. "I was walking along the sea front that very same evening, having just come out of the hospital and I heard a gull cry out and I looked up and right there and then the gull decides to take a shit and it hits me smack in the eye."

"You can't lose an eye from bird shit."

"You can," says John, "when you've just been fitted with a hook for a hand."

I thought it funny. But something had happened to the mood of the audience. They had turned against the acts. The laughter soon ended and battered wives, CEO'S, M.P.'s of all three parties and some Independents, airline stewardesses and a few one-armed bandits joined up with a number of Long John Silver impersonators in the audience and stormed the stage.

The woman comic lasted 4 seconds, tops.

At which point in time, a knight in full armour clanked his way into the Hall and up to the bar. He tells the barman he has this damsel in distress to rescue and his horse has just failed him. Has the barman got a horse? Has anyone the barman knows got a horse? The barman says it's a shame he hadn't called in earlier when Eric was here and that no, he's sorry but he doesn't know of any horse that the knight could borrow. What he does have, however, is a very big dog. And, given the important nature of the knight's task, he'd be more than welcome to take the dog, if he thought it would be of some use. The knight sees this massive Newfoundland standing there behind the bar with a leash in his mouth, wagging his tail, just waiting to be taken out and he cannot resist it. So he climbs up on the dog's back and rides him off into the night amid crashing thunder and vivid lightning.

What a scene is taking place at the tortoise table! The old tortoise is making a complete buffoon of himself. He's screaming and shouting at the top of his ancient lungs. He says that baby tortoise should have been back hours ago, that some ill has obviously befallen him and that they should drink his beer before it gets any flatter. The middle-aged tortoise finally gives up in desperation and the old tortoise, being who and what he is, insists on having the first drink. He lifts baby tortoise's beer to his lips and just as the amber fluid is about to flow into his dry old mouth, a tiny tortoise head pokes round the corner of the door and shouts, "Right! For that! I'm not going!" The old tortoise almost has a coronary, I tell you, and drops the beer into his lap. Collapse, as they say, of stout party.

Meanwhile, onstage, the jokes continue to appall. What would you do, asks this balding man with bulging biceps, if you woke up with carpet burns on your knees and elbows and you've got a condom hanging out of your arse? You wouldn't tell anyone, would you? You wouldn't? Oooo, then, do you want to come camping this weekend?

Up on their feet are bikers, hippies, social workers, dentists, mechanics, model makers, football referees, tattooists, receptionists and a dozen or so born-again Christians. Down goes the comic.

Just then in walks a man with a fish under his arm. He comes up to the bar and explains that he is the owner of Rover, the dog. Rover, it transpires, has been coming in on his own for the last few days since his owner has been away on business and the barman has been good enough to serve Rover drinks and make him feel more than welcome.

"As a token, therefore, of our appreciation for all you've done for Rover," says the man, "I'd like you to have this salmon trout."

"How kind, how generous," says the barman. "I'll take him home for supper when I'm finished here."

"No, don't worry about that," says the man. "He's already had his supper. Just give him a glass of warm milk before bedtime."

Onstage another fight is taking place. This time, it's as a result of the answer to the question: Should a Jew and Arab or a Black fall from a plane without parachutes, who would hit the ground first? Answer: Who cares? This time, it's the turn of anti-vivisectionists, tree-surgeons, marine biologists, headhunters, shoe salesmen and television personalities.

Then the front doors burst open to another crack of thunder and flash of lightning. Following the combined forces of the Dagenham Girl Pipers and the Mormon Tabernacle Choir, comes the knight in armour in a very sorry state, indeed. He's soaking wet, covered in weeds and broken shrubs. His armour has rusted badly, too, and he's painfully dragging behind him a totally exhausted Newfoundland dog.

"Didn't work out, then?" asks the barman.

"Let's put it this way," says the knight. "He's not a fit dog for a knight to be out on. That's all."

The Pipers and the Choir have just completed a most stirring version of "When a body meets a body ..." and a comedian, maybe having witnessed the plight of the Newfoundland, asks what is the kindest dog of all? The audience doesn't know. The hot dog is the answer. Because it feeds the hand that bites it. The audience doesn't care. Butchers, bakers, candlestickmakers, psychoanalysts, charlatans, belt and braces' manufacturers, winners and runners up of beauty contests, hairstylists, transvestites, race car drivers, poets, pregnant women, deep sea divers, an Eskimo, two Serbs and a Croat take to the stage and flail the comic.

Then comes the Grand Finale. The band of the Grenadier Guards, a battalion of Horse Guards and members of the Royal Canadian Military Police take up their places on the stage. After a 21 gun salute, using live ammunition, and one verse of "God Save Our Gracious Queen", the few comedians, pranksters and jokers still in evidence are taken out of the Hall and drowned in the nearby River Nidd beneath a wet and cloudy sky lit bright by fireworks.

Well, it certainly was a big night. A very big night for the little Yorkshire village of Darley and for Jim and myself who left very quietly. We'd had our laughs, we were tired, and we didn't want tears before bedtime.

MERRY MEN IN THEIR MIDDLE AGES

Forget Paramount, MGM, Warner Brothers. Forget Errol Flynn, Basil Rathbone and Olivia de Havilland and Claude Rains. Forget Richard Greene. Forget Sean Connery and Audrey Hepburn and Robert Shaw, though theirs was nice, sad and nice. But no. Not really. No, it's pointless pretending, those days in Sherwood were not a lot of laughs. And they weren't pretty times.

It were not, as they say, all beer and skittles. Not by a long chalk. It were, if anything, wet; it were cold and it were dark for much of the time. You forget that. You don't realise but when you take away electricity and gas and you rely on oil, there's not a lot of light. For a start, of course, there was not a lot of oil. There was tallow and, boy, did that stuff stink! Most of us preferred the dark, to be honest. What we'd have given for an EverReady or Gold-topped Duracell battery I cannot begin to tell you. Not that it would have been much help, mind you.

Life, in short, was tough. And it was short. And you very soon got fed up. You got fed up of the same old food (venison for the most part and very rich at that). That is, if there were food. If not, you got fed up with not having any food. You got fed up with being on the run all the time. Funny expression, "on the run", when you think that we spent most of our time wandering about or sitting on our arses waiting for something to happen. And very little ever did, except for Alan-a-Dale playing his bloody lute. Boy, did you get fed up with Alan-a-Dale playing his bloody lute! You also got mightily fed up with wearing Lincoln Green day in and day out. I don't know which designer came up with that but any one of us Merry Men would cheerfully throttle the bastard if we could get our hands on him.

Like I said, it were a short life and an unhappy one in the main. Not that Robin were a bad man or a bad leader. Don't misunderstand me. Robin were a good man, yes. I liked Robin. Not that he weren't a little misguided, shall we say, at times. A little egocentric. A little overambitious. A little full of his own importance. A little condescending occasionally. A little over demanding, too. But, all in all, a good man. I mean, who's going to argue against robbing the rich? It's what political parties get elected for saying they'll do and never do. Robin did it, that's the difference. And, except for the rich, who's against that? Not me. Not you, I bet.

I quite liked the robbing bit, must say. When we had decent weapons, that is. Pitchforks and ploughshares against spears, halbeards and broadswords isn't my idea of fair play.

But when we were all set, it were fun. It certainly broke the monotony of sitting around looking at the trees of Sherwood and the unwashed faces of each other.

That's background, if you like. I'm sure I don't have to describe in detail the sanitary conditions in camp. There were none. I'm sure I don't have to describe what it's like to wake up in damp clothing on wet earth and try to light a fire with a sodden flint. I mean, these day to day pieces of trivia hardly serve to add much to the scene, do they? And anyway, my story is not about life in Sherwood day to day. It is about the last day in Sherwood. It is about the very end of an age.

What a fiasco! Why the hell he thought he could do it beats me. We all said the same thing. Robin, we said, you are not as young as you used to be. You are not as fit as you used to be. You are not the man you once were. Why choose to go against a man like Nottingham now? Why choose a man-to-man against someone who can afford to pay for professional coaching? Who lives in a very nice house with nice furnishings? Who gets at least 8 full hours sleep at night in a comfortable bed? Who trains every day against pro. sparring partners? Who has a balanced diet and a full gym to work out in? Who has everything going for him save one thing: crowd support? That's one thing he lacks and always has. But then who needs popularity when you're rich and healthy? That's my point.

Talking of health, would you credit it? The day that Robin chooses to accept Nottingham's challenge to a duel is the damn same day Will Scarlet and I have a doctor's appointment. Well, I think, shall I cancel? Not on your life. Our National Health system stunk back then. You had to wait months, years for an appointment. And I was in pretty bad shape. Not as bad as Will, of course, who was still reeling from a very debilitating attack of bubonic plague. It was my feet that was the problem. They were playing me up something rotten because rotten is really very much what they were. Walking around in wet boots doesn't help, you know, day after day after day.

Anyway, Robin's accepted the idiotic challenge and off he goes with this mace he'd borrowed from some old pal of his back from the Crusades and this sword he'd taken from a very aggressive priest who'd stumbled into our camp one day. He was certainly no friend of our fat friar, I can tell you. A nasty piece of work all round. And, like I was saying, Will and I set sail for the local quack, a certain Doctor Vulgaris by name.

So we knock back a few in the Blue Boar Tavern. Well, in those days you had to, there being no anaesthetics of course. What else could you do to ease the pain? The blow to the back of the head with a ball-peen hammer was rarely, if ever, the instantaneous relief it should have been.

Now tell me something. Where do these doctors get their receptionists, eh? In my experience, though limited it is for sure, I have yet to walk into a doctor's reception and not feel a surge in the loins, no matter how bad I'm feeling any where else. Is it the white uniform? The swelling of perfect breasts beneath the tight white nylon. Hips and buttocks testing the fabric to the full? You tell me. Hair always perfect, lips moist and parted, eyes wide and filled with innocence and sympathy, eh? Know what I mean? That's what it were like back then. That's how it always were.

Will and I then, having been rendered almost speechless by

the beauty of Vulgaris' receptionist and almost legless by the potency of the brew at the Blue Boar, had almost forgotten poor Robin. But it must have been around this time that Nottingham landed the first of many blows to our tired and very middle-aged leader. Dear God, the thought of it even now is enough to bring a rush of guilt and remorse. But we did have to tend to the business in hand, especially the business of Will's tests which were back from the lab and, yes, says the divine creature behind the glass partition, the doctor will see us now.

Will, understandably, is nervous. And Vulgaris' bedside manner, as they call it, leaves a lot to be desired. He's a sprightly little chap who can't sit or stand still for a second. He ignores Will and starts in about my feet. Frankly, he tells me there's not a lot he can do about them. It's the damp, no question about it and I'm going to have to try and keep them dry. Otherwise, he informs me they won't be much good to me, "not as feet" as he put it. What as? I can't help but wonder.

That over with, he digs out Will's file. Will's being very quiet and getting darker by the second. I don't like the look of him. Vulgaris doesn't look like he likes what he's reading, either. He's holding the results of Will's tests. It's an early kind of printout, a hard copy of the original illustrated manuscript but very high quality indeed with a particularly well-executed illuminated "W" (for "Will" I guess) in the top left.

"Well, Doc, waddya have ter say?" asks Will, trying not to sound too overly worried. He looks, well, almost black now.

"Mr Scarlet," says the doctor, reaching into his desk and bringing out a decanter of malmsey and some glasses, "have a drink. For I do have some good news and I do have some bad news, Mr. Scarlet." And with that, he pours a large one and hands it to Will. Will downs it.

"Bad news first, eh, Doc." says Will with courage.

"Well, as you probably know, bubonic plague or as it's

becoming better known, Black Death, isn't an easy thing to treat, let alone cure, Mr. Scarlet. Have another drink."

"You mean, Doc, that I'm ... I'm," says Will downing a second glass of malmsey.

"That's precisely what I mean, Will. May I call you Will?"

"So the bad news is, Doc, that I've got what? A year?"

"Er no, Will," says Vulgaris studying the results.

"C'mon, Doc. How long? Six months?" Will really is getting very, very dark.

The doctor shakes his head and pours Will another malmsey and pours one for me too. Then pours one for himself. We all need one, it seems.

"A month? A week? Less than a week? A day?" Will is starting, just starting to flap a bit. The doctor continues to shake his head. The bad news isn't just bad. It's bleeding catastrophic.

"How long, Doc? Less than a day? How long?"

"I'd reckon about 8 minutes. I'm sorry," says the doctor, pouring more drinks.

"Oh, God. Sweet Jesus!" cries Will. He's visibly shaken. I'm shaken. And for once, the doctor doesn't stir.

There's not a lot you can say at such a time. "Well, Will, at least you know. You wanted to know, Will," is the best I can muster. Pitiful, really, looking back on it. But what could I say?

"Right," says Will, whose face is as black as a crow by this time. Quite scarey, actually. And we both get up to leave.

"Again, I'm sorry," says Vulgaris as we reach the door.

"Oh, wait," says Will, remembering something. "Didn't you say you had some good news when we came in?"

"Oh, that. Well, yes," says the doctor as he starts tidying up the glasses.

"Well, Doc ... Well, what is it?" Will needs to know.

"Well," says Vulgaris quite casually, "did you by any chance happen to notice the new girl out on reception?"

"Did we notice?" says I, "How could we not notice?"

"Pretty, don't you think?"
"Not half," says Will and I.
"Fabulous figure."
"Mmmmmmmmm"
"Wonderful personality"
"We believe you, Doc."
"A terrific thinker, too."
"Really, Doc," says Will who realises suddenly that time is not, as they say, on his side. "But what, Doc is the good news?"
"We are having an affair," says Vulgaris. Just like that, with a little smile.
Will topples forward. I catch him. Vulgaris then helps me get him to the examination table. And during this, I cannot help but think about that line about laughter being the best medicine. It's probably right, you know. But Will, poor Will, weren't laughing. Within another few minutes, he weren't breathing or doing much of anything, in truth. 'Twere a wretched business. Ghastly. And that was just the start of it, that day.

Back in Sherwood, there's one hell of a to-do going on. The news of Will's death is quite overshadowed by worse news. For Robin, the day has been a shocker. A real doozy, as we used to say. Proving, of course, that we were right all along: Robin never should have accepted the challenge. He should have asked for a rain-check. It would have been easy enough. Then he could have just kept putting it off and putting it off until Nottingham got tired of asking. But no. Not Robin. And what happened? He was roundly and soundly thrashed. And he's in big trouble.
Ms. Marion is running around like a scalded cat, preparing medications, chicken soup, bread poultices, mustard plasters and all manner of things worthy of a real Florence Nightingale. There's not a dry eye in camp as the word spreads that it looks certain that Robin's a goner. Not a merry man to be seen for

miles around.

Sensing the end to be near, Robin calls his closest friends to his bedside. There's Little John, Friar Tuck, Alan and yours truly all standing in his hut in the forest. It's a fairly makeshift affair but he does have a few nice pieces of furniture. I spot a particularly fine Louis I armoire and a very rare, possibly priceless, William I dresser. And there we are, standing around at a total loss for words, by his bed, an early Harold brass and iron job (quite common at the time though not lacking taste). Robin looks bad.

"Bring me my trusty bow," he calls out, barely audible beneath the bearskin on the bed. "And bring me my quiver." Ms. Marion obliges. She being the only one not blubbering. Funny that, how strong some women can be at such times.

"Now," says Robin, very croakily, "I will fire an arrow and where e'er that arrow lands, there you shall bury me. It is my dying wish, men. See to it."

It broke our hearts I tell you. Tears poured freely now. Shoulders shook, sleeves were soon soggy. My, it were sad. And Ms. Marion handed him his trusty bow and an arrow and tenderly bent to kiss the brow of him, her live-in lover for over 20 years (they never married, you know). Robin took it, summoning all his remaining strength, and placed the arrow on the bow, pulled back the string and let the arrow fly.

We buried him half way up the wall, just above the William I dresser. Ah, me. Ah, my.

THE LAST LAUGH

"O.K. Planet Earth, listen up:
"Why did the chicken cross the road?
"Who was that lady I saw you with last night?
"Where do you weigh whales?
"O.K. President Bush, Mrs. Thatcher, Monsieur Mitterand, Herr Kohl, Mr. Gorbachev, Mr. Shamir, Mr. Arafat, Mr. Botha, Kaunda, Assad, Menem, Ghandhi ... and everyone, my thanks once again for getting together in this way. Really, I cannot thank you enough. And if I didn't think it important, I promise I'd never have asked you. And, of course, I do realise that if you hadn't have thought it important, you wouldn't have done it. I know, I know. And we all know why we're here, right? So .... do we have the answers? Are we ready for a laugh? Are we? I'll give you a minute or so more for translation purposes. O.K.?"

Well, not a bad start. I mean, they all made it. They all introduced themselves to me and to each other. (Well, I presume it was them. I have to believe it though I have to admit that telephones do have their limitations. However.) And they all sounded jolly anxious to get on with things. Well, "anxious" sounds a little harsh, let's say "keen", shall we?

What worries me slightly, along with a whole universe of other things, are the reactions of the Central and South Americans, the South Africans, the Muslims and the Indonesians. Yes, they say they're co-operating. But are they? I mean, have they really turned over their TV and radio stations to this? Have they really tuned out the likes of the Patty Duke Show, Bonanza, Gunsmoke, Mr. Ed, My Three Sons, Sunday Night at the London Palladium, The Prisoner, Lassie and The Cisco Kid? But then again, have the pornographers been unplugged in New York City, L.A., Scandinavia, Italy and Germany? And have game shows been aborted all across America, Europe and the Far East? Have things, in fact, been focused? Focused on this earth-shattering (sic) event? Focused on me?

"Is everybody happy?" I shout, flicking the switch on and off. I like this, I like this a lot, it's great to keep them on their toes.

You see, I worry about us. Us human beings. Really, I do. I mean, I ask you, when was the last time we all had a terrific time together? I mean it: together. When? Eh? When did we last have a laugh, together? When? When was the last laugh we had, together? I, for one, cannot remember. Can you?

Oh yes, we occasionally have communal grief. Occasionally. And, really, how communal? It's usually kind of limited in its appeal, this grief. What I mean by that is, for example, take the assassination of a president. A U.S. president, say. Now, I for one would be hurt, angered, upset and sorry. Others however, may find it cause for rejoicing. They might just sing a few songs, set off a few fireworks and then go out and lob a few mortars in the direction of Beirut or detonate a car bomb in Belfast. Newsreels of starving children in one African state may be good reason for a rethinking of a foreign policy in another part of Africa. Sparking that oh so human trait of greed, coupled with the desire to kick someone while they're down. The spread of disease is something else. A virus laying low millions may bring a flicker of a smile to the lips of millions of others who do not share the first group's politics, social mores, economic policies or religious persuasion.

Hold on there, now. Hold it right there, partner. Jeez. Am I getting serious, or what? What is going on here? Wait a minute. No. No, all I'm saying is that, my God, we are a funny bunch. And, God, if you really did make us in your image, you must be the funniest bugger of all. Which is what gave me this idea in the first place. Once I'd found myself alone, up here, in the one and only Star Wars (as the media used to love to call it) satellite. Another funny thing, that. I mean, after all the fuss, it takes private enterprise to put this thing (with me in it) where it belongs, up here. Hmmm. This and me, ultimate defenders of the Western World, the Free World.

That's what they told me. That's what I told them I believe in. More than myself. More than anything. And, you know something, I did. Yes, I did. I swear. I did. Until I'd been up here for a few weeks. Circling that dear, sweet little ball of blood and faeces, skin, water, rock, metal, go on, go on, name it, name everything we know. As human beings. Then it was, thinking these thoughts, that I had this idea. Wait, the time's up, been up for ages.

"World? Earth? Hi! Well, have we the answers? Do we know them? You bet some of us jokers do. You bet we do. But I'll bet some of us don't. So, this time around, I'll give you the answers, the real answers, O.K? They are.....

"(1) That was no chicken that was my mother-in-law, (2) That was no whale that was my wife and (3) My wife says that it's a whale weigh station, right?

"So do I hear laughter, Earth? Do I? Were your answers wittier than the real ones? Did we laugh and laugh? I want to hear laughter, world leaders. I need to hear it now. Come Mr. B, Mrs. T, Comrade G, come everyone, hold your telephones out of your windows. I want laughter ringing round the world. And I don't hear it, World.

"So now .... what I want now, world leaders, is this. What I want is for you, yes you, to come up with a joke each and I want you to let me and the world have it, O.K? O.K. I'll give you ten minutes to come up with your best joke. That's not hard, for heaven's sake, is it? Am I asking for the moon? No. Just let it be a good one, is all I ask. O.K? Bye for now."

Yeah, like I was saying, it was basically the fact that I cannot remember the last time the human race got together for a laugh or a chuckle or even a titter that gave me this idea. I mean who's in a better position than I to get us together for a giggle, you know? They say humour is universal in its appeal, don't they? They'd better be right. Or ... kerboom, kerboom.

I warned them. And, other than that, if it isn't, I'm really wasting my time. And, come to think of it, the time of some of the most expensive people in the world. People whose time is big bucks. Bucks don't come much bigger than theirs.

And I did explain my own theory to them. I think, you see, that the jokes cannot be sophisticated. They've got to be, well, childlike if not childish. It's got to be kid's stuff, like ... wait, yes, I'll send it down, anyway, what the hell.

"Hi, World. Me again. Don't worry boys and girls at the top, I'm not cutting your precious thinking time, no. It's just that I've come across another teeny weeny ribtickler that may just tickle a few ribs from Valparaiso to Vladivostok, from Adelaide to Anchorage, from Cape Town to Cannes, from Tokyo to Timbuktu. Here goes.... How, World, how ...do you start a teddy bear race?........ Time's up....... Ready, teddy, go! Be back soon."

Oh God, just realised. My own mistake. Exactly what I meant by keeping it simple, you know. And I tell a language joke. Jeez. How stupid. How plainly stupid. God. Am I a fool or what? Well, wait. Maybe that'll help them. Maybe it will assist. Seeing what works and doesn't. Hee hee. Imagine the chaos down there. Teddy bear. Teddy. Ha! Ha! God alone knows what the average Ibo, Eskimo, Iranian, Tibetan, Peruvian or Finn made of that. But isn't it wonderful, being in this position? God, can I begin to tell you how wonderful it is? I mean, yes, it is naughty. Very, very naughty. But, trust me. My heart is in the right place. I'm doing this for the sake of humankind in general. And who can blame me? Who? Don't answer that.

You know what? They say, "Laugh and the world laughs with you" right? Well, I'm going to prove their point. They know, only too well, that this ship is more than equipped to blow away anything anyone sends up against it. It's capable of more than that, too. I could blow away a planet if I wanted to. Earth, sure, no problem. If Earth has a problem and they decide they don't need it they can call and ... kerboom! Just think about that. Think about it. I'm not sure, you know, that they thought about it. Not really. Not when they built this ship and its lasers and warheads and capabilities, no, they didn't think. Especially when they chose me, me, to command it. That's funny. No. No, I know I am being a bit naughty getting all those world leaders together. But why not? Who else could have done it? What can be the harm in that? Even if I fail, what have we lost?

That was a masterstroke, however, though I must say so myself. Getting them to come up with their own jokes. Getting them to make the world laugh. Imagine. Imagine Margaret Thatcher telling a joke that makes a Papua New Guinean fall out of his hammock laughing. Imagine Yassir Arafat getting a little old Jewish grandmother in hysterics of joy. Imagine George Bush having a shopgirl in Baghdad wet her knickers? Imagine. You can't. 'Course you can. That's the point. If it isn't, I'm sunk. I mean, smiling is infectious and what about the power of laughter? Nobody can stop me now. Nobody. Because up here I am invulnerable, unassailable and I can demand what I want.

Wonder what Mrs. T. has come up with. Nothing too English, I hope. Hmm. My favourite English joke doesn't seem to translate at all. It's about a man who goes into a pet shop and asks the assistant, who closely resembles John Cleese in Monty Python mode, for a wasp. John tells him that this is a pet shop, a shop that sells pets, that sells dogs, that sells cats, that sells hamsters, that sells fish, that even sells gerbils. But that does not sell wasps. "Oh, yes you do," says the man, "I saw two or three of them in your window only yesterday." Now if you've never seen an English shop window in the height of summer then, no, I can see how it passes you by. It is a peculiarly English joke. And you're dead in the water telling that world-wide. I hope the redoubtable Margaret realises that.

Take Gorby, too. (Please!) No. Only a famous American joke. That's all. And that is another one. But if he, for example, starts in on food shortages and lines of people queueing for Levis, well, it's not going to go down in Boise, Idaho or Kingston, Jamaica, now is it? And if Bush does one of those smart-ass routines from a comedy club in New York or Los Angeles, forget it, Georgie Boy. Dear me. It's possible. It is.

Why am I getting like this? I mean, aren't these people some of the smartest people on Earth? And if not, aren't they surrounded by some of the smartest people on Earth?

If not, something is dreadfully out of kilter here. And, I see, time is up. Here goes.

"Hi there! Mrs. T (ladies first), Mr. B, Comrade G and all. Hi! Are we ready? Just hope you remembered what I said about keeping it simple. You'd better have. Believe me. O.K? So, who's up first?"

"Hello. Hello up there." It's Mrs. Thatcher. "I say, can you hear me? I don't wish to shout."

"I hear you, Mrs. Thatcher."

"Then I hope you can hear this. Hear it good. We, the leaders of the world, and I, in particular, have a problem. Not that it's a insurmountable problem, Mr. Smith. No problem is, believe me. It's just that we do have a problem. And, your somewhat supercilious attitude isn't helping, Smith. We have a problem with your demands. We in the Conservative Party ..."

Quick. I've got to stop this. It's fast developing into a party political broadcast, for heaven's sake. Well, actually for the sake of the British Conservative Party. I mean, she seems to have totally missed the point.

"Mrs. Thatcher..."

"And one more thing ... "

"Mrs. Thatcher, please."

"... how can we be expected to behave like comedians, comediennes, vaudevillians ... "

"Mrs. Thatcher, please!"

"... when you think of our standing, not only in our countries, but in the world? Our standings, young man. Our positions."

"Mrs. Thatcher!"

"Think, young man. You may have been seconded to the Americans. But you are still a Brit. And I believe, there has to be some common decency left in you. There has to be."

"Mrs. Thatch..."

"Think of it, Smith. It may be foreign money that got you up there. But where will you come home to? Ask yourself that Mr. Henry Smith."

"Tell him, Maggie." That must be Mulroney, or Bush or maybe, yes, that Aussie fellow.

"Just listen to me," I say. "I am very serious about this. You know who I am, you know where I am and you know what I and this infernal machine can do. Now don't you?"

Silence.

"Knowing that, all you have to do, now that we're all together ..... Catholic, Protestant, Shiite, Buddhist, Sikh, Sophist, you name it, you got it ... now we're here, as it were, we're going to have a good time. I want us, the entire world, to have a good laugh. And who better to do that than the likes of you Mr. Qaddafi, you Mrs. Ghandi, you Generals Noriega and Castro ..? I mean, you can do it, pals. You can."

"Mister Smith...." It's Mrs. T. again. "You obviously haven't been paying attention." God, is this woman insufferable, or what? I know now what TV interviewers talked about.

"Margaret," I say.

"Mister Smith ... how can we tell .. jokes? How? Think about it. How can we tell jokes without political, without economic, without social, without religious overtones and implications? Believe me, Mr. Smith, we've talked it over carefully, Mr. Smith. Carefully. And ... it's quite ... impossible."

"Margaret, if I may call you that, if I may continue," says George Bush. "Listen Henry, can I call you 'Hank'? Think about it, son. Think about the minorities."

I can't take any more of this. "Mr. Bush, look up into the sky. It's night with you, right? What do you see, Mr. Bush? You see, Mr. Bush, let me tell you, a thousand points of light, Mr. Bush. I'm one of them. Your friends made me one of them, Mr. Bush. And, now that I'm one of them, Mr. Bush, I call the shots. And please don't call me 'Hank'."

"You have to understand, Henry," says Bush but gets no further. A thousand voices in as many tongues intercept him and fill the airwaves. It's a cacophonous nightmare.

"SILENCE!" I scream. The Babel-like babble subsides.

"Monsieur Smith," says (I presume) Monsieur Mitterand "what Madame Thatcher and President Ford, forgive, Bush, I believe are trying to say is true. C'est vrai. We cannot."

Jeez, what is this? What the hell is going on here?

C'mon, who's runnin' this show? "You can. You will."

"We cannot, Comrade Smith. We will not." Good Lord, it's Gorby.

"Why the hell not, Mikhail? Eh?"

"Because it simply will not work," says Gorbachev.

"What!!! You cowards!!!" I cannot believe this.

"Hank, Henry, be reasonable, son. Put the gun away. Let's be reasonable. Let's get back to doing what we're supposed to be doing. What we're paid to do. Let's just run our countries, for Christ's sake."

Sweat has formed across my entire face. I cannot take this nonsense. "Wait," I say. "Wait. Isn't it true that you 'laugh and the world laughs with you'? If you did that, if you all did that, then, think ... think."

"Happiness, an Irish Archbishop once said, is no laughing matter," says Kenneth Kaunda. Which is O.K. for him to say, I think.

"And that's a joke in itself," I say. I'm panicking. I mean, listen, did I tell them? Or did I tell them? I told them. They had the option.

"Can't be done, my friend," says Mr. Bush.

"Simple as that," says, I think, Herr Kohl.

"WAIT A MINUTE," I shout. What's got into these people? "Laugh and the world laughs with you, right?"

"And the next part of the saying, Mr. Smith?" says that Thatcher person, adding "Good-bye" in a voice with the depth of Paul Robeson.

"WAIT!" This cannot be happening it can't because I warned them I gave the option I told them I told them I told them they know what I am capable of what this ship is capable of what we can do and I will I will I will I will I will why am I crying why I can and I will why am I so alone why am I in tears why do I feel so lonely why, for heaven's sake, oh why why why I will I will I will I can I can I can.

"Goodbye, Mr. Smith," says Herr Kohl.

"Goodbye, Henry and good luck. And keep up the good work. The West, the Free World is relying on you, Henry. Never forget that, Henry. We never do. Take care, now. And thanks for all you've done for us, so far," says George Bush, I think.

"Bye, bye, au'voir, goodnight, see ya, sport, fare thee well, adios." So it goes, on and on as each of them are saying it is over. It can't be over. They're telling me it is.

"WAIT!" I shout again, too late. They have gone. Why am I crying? Why am I so lonely? Why am I here? Why are we here? Why didn't they ..? Shall I? Shall I? Shall I?........ Shall I? Why? Why not?

TRUE COLOURS

Blimey, you should have seen us by the time we all got together down there in the South of France. What a bunch! Really. I tell you, we really was a very, very mixed bag. We had Africans which you'd expect, seeing as how we was supposed to be a Carthaginian army, right. We had Spaniards which was fair enough since we'd (I say "we" but I mean "he") conquered Spain some time ago. And we had Gauls and yet we are officially still at war with Gaul. And what's truly amazing is how well we all seemed to get along.

I'm talking big numbers, here. There's 80,000 according to this Nielsen geezer, others put us nearer the 60 mark. Either way, that's no small army. It's the size of a town, for heaven's sake. On top of that, there's supposed to be 9,000 or so horses. A lot of geegees, I'd say that was. And then there's us elephants. 38 of us at the time. And we're regarded as the heavy armour. The tank corps, if you like. And, I tell you, we did cause the odd raised eyebrow, especially going through these little places on the Riviera. Funny that, they think nothing about walking about stark bollock naked. But send a troop of us through town and you should hear 'em tut tutting, drawing in the breath through their teeth and shaking their heads. Certainly put paid to a few games of boules we did and caused the bottle or two of Pastis to spill. You'd think we were from another planet, the way some of these people looked at us. Ignorance is all it is, you know. I mean, what do they know about the world? Nothing, that's what.

Me, on the other hand, well, I've seen a thing or two. I have, as my resumé puts it, "travelled extensively". Don't misunderstand me, now. I'm not trying to be smart or nothing. It's fortuitous is what it is. No, let me explain. Won't take a moment.

It was, when was it now? Back in 233 when I was a kid of two and my present guv'nor, Hannibal, would have been fourteen right. Yeah, me and me old Mum had been working for a time for these Chipperfield people in Londinium. Circus folk, you've heard of them. Anyhow, that's where I picked up the old banter, the accent you know. Cor, you should have heard me then. My language, dear oh dear oh dear. I was a shocker. And I'm not just talking the "apples and pears for stairs" kind of slang and the "luv a duck" and the "gor, blimey, darlin'," I'm talking language. But I was a kid and you grow out of that stuff, don't you? If you want to, you do. And, of course, travel helps you do that.

While I was there, most I ever did, besides swear, was to stand with me front two feet on a painted barrel and I'd hold a ball or something equally stupid in me trunk. The crowd loved it. Bleeding daft, I call it. And sometimes Mum and I would play catch which was sort of all right. Then the piece de resistance (as these Gauls will have it) was for us to fill up with good old agua and spray the audience. That made up for everything. What a hoot!

Then we went on the road and you know what it's like on the road. You've heard from bands and people. Well, it's everything they say it is, I tell you. Sleeping in lousy motel rooms and places you wouldn't normally be seen dead in and where you're surprised to wake up and find out you're not (dead that is). And the food. I mean, I know the Angles aren't exactly world bleedin' famous for their culinary expertise but out there ... forget it. Is it junk or is it junk? On top of which there's problems like laundry and stuff and you're living out of a suitcase (no, no, no trunk jokes please) and everything gets creased and has that strange odour, you know.

Anyhow, we're in this dump called Barcelona or something. It were just one hovel, then the next, then the next. A kind of collection of rubbish, really, that people lived in. But it didn't matter as it happened. Because, before we'd even set up the Big Top, Hannibal, Big H himself, turns up and blow me if he doesn't raze the entire place and his elephant Master-Sergeant recruits me and me Mum: sort of press gangs us into service with the 37 other lads he's brought all the way from Numidia (Algeria, to you).

Me Mum didn't last five minutes. No, tell a lie. But you know what I mean. And no, not for that reason. For this reason: when there's a war on (and these days, there's always a war on) your normal morality tends to go out the window. I mean, you can't blame anyone. You never know, you could be dead tomorrow and usually you are, so what the hell? Well, couple that with the fact that these lads from Numidia haven't seen a female of the species since they left home and you'll pretty soon get the idea. They did, I tell you. And then there's me Mum, of course, who probably hasn't seen a man since before I were born. Now you get the idea, right. And that was that, fait accompli and job done. And she went, passed away she did. She went the way many dream of going: with a smile on her lips that looked a mile wide. I felt no sorrow. Not for her. For myself I did but you soon get over that in wartime.

This chap, Hannibal is some fella. They say his dad were a bit on the special side, too. Maybe even more so, but who's to say? I remember me Mum talking about him (how could I forget). What a handle he had. You know his name? Hamilcar Barca. I mean, give over. What kind of name is that? First time I heard it I thought, hold up, what's this, some kind of dyslexic variation on a place of refreshments on British Rail. No, I'm serious. Then I think, wait, hang on there, it sounds like someone who works in a fairground. You know, the geezer who calls the shots on the dodgem cars or what have you. But then, I'm serious I tell you, I think no, it's one of them names you hear at Crufts or the Westminster Dog Show. Turns out it's the name of one of the greatest generals who ever lived, that's who. And who, it turns out, is the father of the man who's my guv'nor today.

Funny old world, isn't it?

Where was I? Don't tell me. I'm the one who is supposed to remember, remember. We was on our way to Rome that's where. That's where we was, with the funniest and largest bunch of men I'd ever clapped eyes on. And, like I said, it was quite amazing to me how soon everyone made friends. Problems of customs, of language were almost instantly overcome. Maybe the ordeals we had to face was what brought us together. I've heard that can happen. Think about it. First, we had to get through the Pyrenees, bloody chilly it was too. And hard going. Then we hit the area round Carcassonne which on a map looks pretty flat. I tell you, I've learned something about maps. Things are never what they look like on the map. There is no such thing as a plain. There is no such thing as flat in reality. On the map, oh yes, oh yes. In real life? No way.

Then there were rivers to cross. This proved no great problem until, you guessed it, we hit the Rhone. By God, is that a big bugger, or what? Jeez, it was tricky.

Then came the really Big One. Or Big Ones, should I say? Oh yeah, we knew they was there. It wasn't like a surprise or something. No. It wasn't that. It was what it was. The Alps. And, I have to tell you, I did begin to wonder, you know, if Big H hadn't gone completely off his bleedin' rocker. Have you seen the size of those mountains? Have you? Big isn't a big enough word. And, of course, there were no roads. I mean, nobody had ever tried to do anything like what we're doing before. And I know why, believe me. So we built roads. Yes, we did. Just to get all these men and all these horses and all of us over some of the highest mountains in the known universe to do what? Yes. Yes, yes, yes. To do what? To meet an enemy and do battle with him. Fella by the name of Scipio, and thousands upon thousands of ready, rested and waiting Roman soldiers. Crazy? I thought so. I had no doubts. I thought Big H had gone, like we used to say, Radio Rental (not right in the head, a little bit or a lot bit mental).

It was around this time that the jokes started. No accident I would surmise. I think Hannibal himself encouraged them. A clever manoeuvre in morale. And it starts with jokes about the

enemy. Things like what airline has planes with hair under
their wings? Alitalia. Like how many gears has an Italian
tank? Six. One forward, five reverse. You know the kind of
stuff. Morale building. Wartime guff. Then they moved on to
jokes about each other. About the black Africans; about sex.
About the women of Gaul; about sex. About sex. About sex
again and, with a quick and none too intellectual skirmish,
about Roman men and Roman men. And, yeah, it had to
happen, inevitable it was. Finally, jokes about us. Which, let
me tell you, was the first time I'd ever heard the like. Never
before had I heard one joke about an elephant. Never, until we
was half way across the Alps that spring.

What's the difference, I hear this Spanish NCO ask a
Numidian cavalry officer, between an elephant and a mail box?
I don't know says the Numidian. Well, says the Spaniard, I
must remember never to ask you to post a letter. Funnee! But
it was that kind of stuff that kept everyone going (along with a
tacit understanding that if you were caught messing about you'd
be put to the sword instantly). And, fact is, we made it.
Though, if you ask me, it was just in the nick of time. I mean,
aside from the freezing winds, the early snows, the late snows,
the avalanches, the sporadic attacks from mad mountain bandit
groups, the sheer ice, and the sheer audacity of attempting it in
the first place, the jokes were wearing thin.

They were down to stuff like how do you hide an elephant
in a bowl of custard? You ask him to lie on his back and you
paint the soles of his feet yellow. Talk about clutching at
straws for laughs here. Blimey. I tell you, it was like the
gubbins you read in those women's magazines for
"homemakers" or whatever housewives and mothers are chosen
to be called these days. You know the magazines I'm talking
about, that go out of their way, go to the ends of the earth and
beyond to be middle-of-the-road, to not offend, to be really
coy. They make my bleedin' toes curl under, I tell you
straight.

You know it's like what's the difference between an

elephant and a raspberry?

I don't know. What is the difference between an elephant and a raspberry?

Well, an elephant is grey and a raspberry is red.

Ho, bleeding ho, is what I say. But then, we had been through an awful lot, you understand. It was a nightmare up there, in truth, it was. And we'd lost a lot of men and horses and a few of us, too. I'm sad to say. Terrible, really. In fact (Nielsen, again) we had lost close to half our numbers. A fact that certainly helps account for the falling off of quality of the joke telling.

But those of us who made it made it. And we're here in Italia, right. And the sun's out and it's September, I believe, 218, and it's really great being back down where I believe we belong, not far from sea level. At which precise moment we run smack into Scipio and his troops by the River Trebia. Sounds like the name of a Japanese car, don't it?

Well, as you know if you know anything about the history of this period, we gave him a right royal pasting. We wiped the floor with the man as we then went on to do with this Gaius Flaminus (another of those very little men who sincerely believe they are Napoleon or God or both). You know the sort. But one thing we never did do and it still hurts me to think about it. We went all that way, endured all those hardships and yet we never got to see Rome. Really pisses me off, to this day. It was this geezer by the name of Quintus Fabius Maximus who put the ky-bosh on it. He was also known as Cunctator (which you've got to be a bit careful about when putting him in the word processor) which means the Great Delayer. And, jeez, did he know how to delay. He simply sat back, you know, and let us wear ourselves out looking for food and ammunition before we went on to kill over 85,000 (yes, can you believe that, 85,000) Roman soldiers at this place called Cannae. Again, I'm relying on Nielsen but I tell you I've never seen more dead people in my entire life. Then, of all things, Hannibal's brother turns up in Italia and tries to help and immediately gets himself killed. His name if you're interested was, wait for it, Hasdrubal. I mean, where do they get these names? Then what happens? We all get recalled to Carthage. I think the funds had run out. As usual, it was ultimately a question of the bleedin' bottom line.

So I never did get to see the Eternal City, as they call it. Pity, that. Still, I'm past it now. One funny thing, though, I'll never forget for the life of me. You know when we was on our way to Cannae to meet that Fabius fella, you know what I heard? I heard what Fabius said when he first saw us coming over the horizon.

He said, "Look! Here they come! Here come the raspberries!" He was colour blind. And, more than likely, an avid reader of Family Circle.